THE SLED
& other Stories

MARTIN J. REINECKE

[signature: Martin J. Reinecke]

Copyright © 1999
MARTIN J. REINECKE

ALL RIGHTS RESERVED
This work may not be used in any form,
or reproduced by any means, in whole or in part,
without written permission from the publisher.

LCCN: 99-91388

ISBN: 1-57579-174-9

First Printing: October 1999
Second Printing: December 1999

Printed in the United States of America

PINE HILL PRESS, INC.
Freeman, S. Dak. 57029

Dedicated
To the memory of
My Father and my Mother

To the help and patience of my wife
Alma

To my Children
Mary, Hannelore and Max

And to my niece
Margaret

TABLE OF CONTENTS

Foreword vii
Preface ix
Feldt's School and the Flu 1
The Year in Calgary 4
Back in Iowa 10
The Sled 16
Shattered Hopes 20
The Truants 25
Harry and the National Anthem 31
Feeding the Birds 36
A Dog's Day in Court 39
Our Anniversary 44
The Iron 48
The Rag Family – An Allegory 51
Vatch, Mietze and a Goose 56
Waiting for the Mail 60
The False Bottom 66
Good Samaritans 71
Three Vignettes 75
True Gifts 81
All Aboard 83
The Last Parsonage 93
Christmas at Home 100
Anecdotes 104

FOREWORD

Martin and Alma Reinecke have been neighbors of my wife, Mary, and me for over 33 years. We have watched them raise their two youngest children, celebrated birthdays with them and watched them both retire from teaching while continuing to be active participants in both their church and in the community. They are an outstanding and exceptional couple.

Many years ago, we received the first of Martin's Christmas stories. We have read each and every one of his stories with great interest. Most of them are based on the memory of Martin, himself, but a few are based on stories he heard from former generations. Martin says they are all factual and not embellished. My personal experience is that the stories that I have repeated over the years somehow improve with age. Regardless, they are enjoyable, educational and make good reading.

Martin has now agreed, pursuant to request, to publish all of his letters so that his family and friends in the future can look back and enjoy them. I'm glad he did. His children, grandchildren and beyond will be delighted that he did so. They are indeed a treasure of both family and South Dakota history.

Martin and Alma decided to call this compilation "The Sled" after their favorite story, (Christmas 1982). My favorite is the story of the mongrel dog's appearance in South Dakota Circuit Court, (Christmas 1987). I have re-read it several times and it always makes me laugh. It was published in the <u>South Dakota Barrister</u>. I would guess that different readers will have different favorite letters, but that everyone who reads them will be pleased that they did.

David V. Vrooman

It was an Advent afternoon when I came home from work and found my wife, sitting in the rocking chair, and in tears. One of those "Christmas letters" had arrived and she told me I had to sit down and read it. Now! When I finished reading Martin Reinecke's "The Sled" I was in tears, too! What a gift!

The stories of which Martin writes are not nostalgia; they are reminders of the values of faith, family and love which many of us grew up with, but have long since abandoned in this sophisticated age. However, these stories have the ability to awaken in us a spirit of community that gives us hope. Especially, they should be shared with the little ones among us.

I commend this book to you. May it arouse in you your own Christmas memories, and re-kindle in you the joy of sharing. Thank you, Martin: Writer, Teacher, Friend!

Pastor Steven Molin
August 15, 1999

PREFACE

When I was growing up, my mother taught me to write and to correspond with my cousins in Ohio by mail. It was the only way I had of getting acquainted with my relatives. After I left home for college, letters to my parents became very numerous. For a three-cent stamp I could send several pages of writing. Telephones were used only in emergencies.

I thought that sending cards for any specific celebration or occasion with just my signature was not a sincerely sufficient greeting, so I began to add personal notes to them. My notes and letters became a biography of memories from the passing years of my youth.

In 1977 I began to center my Christmas greeting around a specific event, expanding it into a story. Readers expressed favorable comments on that development. Every year since then, I have sent my Christmas greeting with a story. My family and friends requested that I make the stories available in a book.

These stories, anecdotes and vignettes express the tempo of my life growing up a preacher's son.

Martin Reinecke

FELDT'S SCHOOL AND THE FLU

When Christmas comes, I find that it is not easy to stop at reflections of the past year. This year, 1978, ought to remind us of and call our attention to the sadness that hung over our land 60 years ago. It marked the end of the Great War. A month ago we celebrated Armistice Day. But the time also brought on the great Flu Epidemic. My experience as a nine-year old boy was shared by millions of others.

* * *

After the four of us had gotten into the buggy-sled that morning, my oldest sister said, "Giddyup," and our horse Teddy trotted swiftly for two miles. Today was a special day. Sunday clothes were suited to anxious expectations The festive spirit excused any mishaps and sheer joy prevailed. After several last minute rehearsals, we settled into our designated places and eagerly awaited the arrival of our parents for this was the day of the Christmas Program. People filled the room until there was no room for movement, but no matter. Great things always move and the program went on. The singing, the dialogues, the skits, the goodies in the brown sacks, the visiting among neighbors and the merry-making were sure signs that it was Christmas! It was also the last day before vacation at Feldt's School in Mitchell County, Iowa. Augusta Doescher was the teacher.

That evening the cold in our upstairs rooms didn't bother us as we went to bed after a few last comments on the events of the day. But the next morning brought symptoms of aches which became groans, pain, fever and vomiting as the day passed. One after another, we all grew weak and faint, victims of a silent destroyer. Only Papa remained on his feet.

A bed was set up in the parlor where the hard coal heater was. Another bed was set up in the adjoining study. Mama and the baby were to stay in the bedroom and I was on the couch. With this arrangement all seven of us could most easily be monitored and ministered to.

Outside it was cold and the snow grew deeper. Teddy and the cow and chickens needed attention, too. Mama developed pneumonia and was delirious for many days. When she would ask one of us whether we still had our "pocketbook" Papa would calm her with a proper disguise by answering "Ja" for each of us.

In the youngest children, Whooping Cough became most severe. We could hear Papa plead and pray when he tried to help our baby sister as she began turning blue during her spasms. The telephone allowed us to keep in touch with the outside world, but the news was grim. Papa was often called for pastoral care. He conducted funeral services for his best friend who had seen two of his children die just days before. We heard the jingle of the harness bells as the bobsled with the casket went past our house. Neighboring farmers still on their feet would make the rounds once a day, doling out food and bread and a doctor came through our rooms once wearing a white mask. But Papa, without a change of clothes during the siege, seemed inexhaustible save for one lapse when he fell asleep after opening the draft on the heater. We were awakened by his shout and cry in a room lighted brightly from the hot orange flicker of the stove that was in full glow its entire length into the chimney.

Happiness returned again as one after the other we were declared "out of danger." Mama was the last to regain her strength and it was some time in January when the eight of us were all able to be together for supper. That was a solemn, though happy, occasion. After a prayer of thanksgiving and offering special thanks for our personal preservation, Papa said "this is our Christmas." A branch of the unused tree intended for the church stood in the corner of the kitchen where we sat.

✳ ✳ ✳

Wise men of today, especially those who are exploring the intricacies of the mind and the brain, together with those who are searching in the infinity of our physical nature, are concluding that there is a "Good" of some kind, be it organic or inorganic, that is responsible for the make-up of our universe. They have used the word "Love" interchangeably in explaining the term "Good." Years ago I learned a verse which I may not remember exactly, but what has stayed in my mind is "God is Love, and whoever abides in Love abides in God and God in him."

The Birthday of the incarnation of Love in the form of Jesus should renew hope in the hearts of us all.

> *During the 1920's, right after the war, there were a lot of hard feelings between people of German descent and every other group. I was aware of much ridicule, but thought it was a normal thing. But I could gather that my dad's feelings about this were much deeper. Germans tried to show patriotism by demanding Sunday services in English, though they were not able to understand any of the language. Nobody wanted to have his church or parsonage painted yellow during the night. Yellow was the sign of a slacker.*

THE YEAR IN CALGARY

"Yes, we have a house for you," was the positive reply that Papa was waiting for. It filled the family with anticipation, for now we would move to Canada. I was very young, but I could understand "far away." We delayed our departure after the furniture had left, to be sure that it would arrive in Calgary ahead of us. When the telegram came saying it was there, we lost no time in following.

What made Papa decide to take the call which would add another 1,400 miles to the distance from Mama's relatives in Ohio? Could this have been the answer to his original desire and call which took him to the seminary in Hermannsburg twenty years ago, to spend seven years there in preparation for work in the mission fields of India?

It did not take long to have the furniture brought in and arranged. Joy was abundant when Papa asked for the Lord's blessing on the new home in which we would live. But the happiness and enthusiasm were not to last long. After only a day or two, the house was proven to be infested with bed bugs. As speedily as things were moved in, they were now moved outside into the front yard. If it had not been for Papa, who was going about the entire display of the family's worldly goods with a vintage pump spray filled with kerosene of which he gave everything a good measure, the display looked as though it was being readied for an auction sale. Mama cried and said "That smell will last for a long time."

I heard Papa say "None of these things will ever go back into that house." Another place must be found, now, one in which people could live. After that, it did not take long for dray wagons to come. The men loaded everything and moved it to a large house on the high east side overlooking the Bow River. The scene stretched west for 40 miles in prelude to the Rocky Mountains. The view from the window on the west side of the house allowed us to see the whole world, or so I thought. Below us were the river, the bridge and the railroad tracks with big engines belching black smoke. There were whistles and buildings with tall chimneys. But beyond all this activity, the countryside was brown, extending as far as one could see. I did not yet have reason enough to catch the grandeur and magnitude of the picture, but with helpful descriptions from my older sisters, Johanna and Clara, who pointed out in the distance the mountain peaks of Joffre, Baldwin and Assiniboine, I thought I could see a large cradle between our house on the hill and the mountains out there.

As beautiful as the sights through that window had been, the landscape was entirely changed during just one night. The entire expanse to the right and to the left and as far out as one could see had been covered with a thick coat of snow which had hidden all of our landmarks. Those three peaks out there easily blended in with the eternity of the background, but they showed up well as silhouettes when the sun was setting, leaving an orange glow on the snow on my cradle. It was an entirely new picture. Although our main points of reference were covered, I noticed a black spot a long way out. Papa told me that it was a black bear sleeping.

We certainly were enjoying this house. It even had a back porch with a balcony. For the first time we had running water, a bathroom and a toilet in the house. Such things made life easier, but they also made it possible to change a person's mood quickly; for instance there was fright and consternation for Mama when she had to call for help because one of the baby's diapers slipped from her grip as she was rinsing it in the stool and pulling the chain to release water from the wooden tank above, both at the same time.

One day, some time before Christmas, Papa and Mama took me along on a ride to the Hudson Bay store. I was told that I would get to play in a large park on the roof. Although my sisters had made me a bit apprehensive, I said I would not be afraid even though I had never been left alone, let alone left with strangers. Mama's kiss must have been a bit more tender than usual, because she quickly turned while Papa took me to a huge door out of which came a great number of people. We entered what I thought was a room. With a bang, the door shut. I kept a firm grip on Papa's thumb while he held me by the hand. The noise, the rattle, the talk and a faint smell, but especially the push and squeeze, didn't allow for any communication between Papa and me, except that I knew he had hold of my hand.

Suddenly, the whole room came to a jerky stop. The large doors opened and Papa took me to a desk where a kind lady tied a tag (Zettel) to my shirt button from which she tore the bottom half and gave to Papa. I was not very aware of Papa's kiss and goodbye. What I saw was too much for me. I stood still and wondered at the swings and slides, the fun and laughter of many children. It really was a play yard and though they said it was on the roof of the tall Hudson Bay Building, I doubted it because I knew that trees grow on the ground, not on a roof. Too soon for me, the kind lady came and brought me to the desk where Mama now stood waiting for me. She had the piece that matched my torn tag. She took me to the lift, not a room as I had thought, and this time we would go down. Papa was there with some bundles and a large sack. I could hardly wait to tell my sisters of the sheep and shepherds I had seen with a star on one side. Papa and Mama told all of us that they had talked with das Christkind.

Christmas was coming, but it came quietly. We were busy learning our verses and songs. Only das Christkind brought gifts. We children did not give gifts to each other. After the program on Christmas Eve, Christkind would come to visit our house, too. When Papa and my sisters came home from the program, and we had patiently waited to have our own little program around the tree with the gifts, there came a loud knock at the door. This couldn't be das Christkind, could it? No, it was just a friend, Mr. Repp. He had a package of two ducks for Mama "for your Christmas dinner tomorrow." Then he sat down to talk. Maybe Mr. Repp saw Mama's chagrin as she gritted her teeth when he reached into his black duck pants pocket to bring out peppermint candies for each of us, because he left shortly after that.

Expectations were great when Papa came into the kitchen to lead the older sisters, my younger sister, Hattie, and me into the living room where, off to one side of the big window, stood a beautiful little tree, around which das Christkind had placed seven groups of gifts. He did not forget Mama and Papa, not even our baby brother, Erwin, who was asleep in the cradle. There was a new set of colors for me, drawing paper and pencils, stockings and underwear, a sack of candy and nuts, an orange and a book! What a great Christmas das Christkind provides!

On Christmas Day, Mama washed the ducks and began to get ready for dinner. Because it was too cold to play outside and because our house was large enough, there were always some neighborhood boys in to play with me. On that day, a friend named Phillip was playing a game on my new paper with me. Because Mama did not want to send him home, she invited Phillip to eat this festive Christmas dinner with us. The table was appropriately set with a pure white spread of table linen and seven place settings. The polished silverware glistened on the white napkins. There was also a place for Phillip. After grace had been said, Mama started the food to be passed around and helped both of us boys to good portions of everything. But Phillip sat there quietly, not touching his food. Mama went to Phillip and asked him what was the matter. He looked up at her and said, "I don't know how to eat here." After some help with the fork and spoon, nothing more was said about it at the table.

The first balloon I ever saw was through our window. That man wanted to cross the river, but had to land midway atop the bridge. We watched that ride through Papa's telescope.

One night after my sisters and I had gone upstairs and were getting ready for bed, we heard a prowler in the hall and then in Papa's study. One sister stayed with me and the other ran downstairs to alert Papa. When he came up and passed my door, I saw him carrying a shingler's hatchet held high in search of the intruder. Then we heard a loud bang as the burglar escaped through the door to the balcony over the back porch. From there he must have slid down one of the posts for we saw his foot prints there in the snow the next morning.

Because the winter was cold, most of my activity was in the house. Boys of the neighborhood liked to spend time in our home with me because sometimes Mama had cookies. But when spring came, we could again go outside and try our muscles at wrestling. Even then, groups of boys like this did not stay in one place. We wandered about the neighborhood and even out of it. One time the group I was with got so far away that Mama could no longer reach me when she called. She thought I was lost, and I was. I could not have found my way home late that afternoon. This event stands out especially because that night Mama discovered that I needed my hair rinsed with kerosene. A lively family of head lice had nested in my hair.

People had trouble with their developing young ones then, too. If Papa were writing this story, he would not miss the episode of the mother who came to him one afternoon with her very young, pregnant teen-age daughter and her boyfriend. The mother wanted Papa to marry the two right there that afternoon. Papa agreed to help her get that done, but first the boy should learn something about the Lutheran tradition; he should be baptized and learn to pray the Lord's prayer, all of which could be done in only a few weeks. But the mother became irritated and impatient with such a delay and declared, "It could go faster just for once, couldn't it?" Of course, I was not a witness to this meeting, but the words "...for once go faster," have been a family expression at appropriate times ever since.

By the time pasque flowers were in bloom everywhere, Papa had assessed the world's political situation and believed that it was ready to explode. Great Britain and Germany were drawing their swords in a round-about way, and he was certain that there would be war soon. Wisdom would advise him, he was sure, that for the protection of himself and his family, he should return to the United States where he was a citizen rather than stay in Canada where he was a foreigner. Arrangements for the move were made in March.

My life in Calgary was over, but as young as I was, the memories linger on. I remember the scenic grandeur through our window as we sat at our beautiful Christmas table while Mama helped my friend Phillip use his fork. I recall the black spot in the distance, though it really wasn't a bear at all. Black water tanks in the distance have been known as bears to our family ever since.

> *The social life of a pastor's family consisted of meeting with members of the congregation, either at some church sponsored affair or private visits or dinners with individual members. The wives of the pastors worked with the Ladies Aid or the Auxiliary and in general refrained from taking part in any congregational affairs, such as elections or decisions at annual meetings. During church services, women sat on the left side of the middle aisle, and men used the right side. Those things changed slowly after women achieved equality with the 19th Amendment.*

BACK IN IOWA

There she sat with four children tugging at her long dress. A large canvas travel bag and a bundle of clothing held together with a piece of bedding was on the floor before them. The children were apprehensive. Although they were quiet and orderly, they were wondering where their father had gone among the hundreds of people in this large Minneapolis Railroad Terminal of the Soo Line. Amid the echoes and din of the huge waiting room only the closest passers-by could hear the soft murmur of the lullaby she was singing to the child on her lap.

"Wo ist der Papa?" asked the children.

Yes, Papa had left them for a little while and they were getting a bit hungry. In this large, strange place which was full of the smell of belching locomotives, nothing could be more welcome at this moment than the sight of their Papa. Soon their happiness exploded as he came out of the crowd in front of them. He was carrying a sack, from which he drew delicacies to eat — some buns and some oranges.

This stop-over for a change of trains was really a happier time for Mama and Papa than it seemed, for we were returning to Iowa, to a parish less than 50 miles from Boyd where brother Erwin had been born. We were coming back from Calgary, Canada, where Papa had been called for service in the German Lutheran Missions for the past year and a half. Sensing a coming of war between England and Germany, he had opted to return to the United States as soon as possible. Life, he thought, would be less threatening in the States where he was a citizen than in Canada, where he would be a foreigner and of German descent besides.

We were very lucky to cross the border just two days before war was declared and World War I began. Had we been delayed until after June 28, we would most likely have been detained for some time, possibly for the duration. Our household goods, which in those days were shipped as freight, were loaded into a railroad box car and were delayed long enough to miss making it across the border in time. There was plenty of time for the border guards to do a thorough job of ransacking our belongings and causing damage while opening crates of breakables in their eagerness.

The Rock Creek Parish, to which we had now come, was exceptional among rural parishes at that time. Papa and Mama were full of great hope and expectations. There were three doors to the house and two large doors to the church which were reachable and connected by cement walks. There was even a cement walk to the outhouse. No wooden walks anywhere! Here there would be chickens, a turkey or two and a cow once again. There was a garden and trees for a swing! What a place!

* * *

When Papa was five years old, his father sold the small farm plot on which they had lived because he could no longer bear to live in the house where all of his children except one, and their mother had been taken in a diphtheria epidemic. After this tragedy, Grandfather became an itinerant cabinet maker and took Papa with him whenever possible. And so it was that Papa did not get much experience in the use of farm animals as a boy. But now, having had an opportunity to learn a few things about handling horses in previous parishes, Papa believed he would be more satisfied if he could drive a horse that was a bit faster and more showy than the nags he had owned before. He became easy game for the horse breeders near the Mason City race track. One of them sold Papa a beautiful, frisky trotter. The trotter was a fine horse, tall and lanky. He was a dandy and his name was Dan! What a big satisfaction it was to hitch this horse to a black, spring buggy! No more simple buckboard now!

* * *

A year had gone by. Because Mama needed some dental work done, Dan was casually hitched to the top-buggy that morning.

After Papa, Mama and I had gotten aboard, Johanna, Clara, Hattie and Erwin waved us a loud good-bye as we drove off. It was a beautiful day and Dan was trotting in stylish fashion. Suddenly, Dan reared up, and spinning around for a complete 180 degrees, he whipped that buggy around so fast between the guard rails of a little bridge that the three of us were thrown free from the buggy. Mama and I were soon on our feet, but Papa could not get up. He could only moan and sob. He had never made such a sound before and Mama began to cry. Papa's face was covered with blood. It was a terrible sight! Mama was tearing pieces from her clothes with which she tried to wipe away and control some of the blood. What else could be done? We were alone.

Meanwhile, Dan had taken off in a wild gallop, dragging the buggy until it came loose. Dan lost the buggy when he was half way to the next farm, where he came to a halt at the gate. That was the alert that brought help. Those people came and brought us to their house. A doctor had been called and arrangements were being made in the kitchen. Papa received much sympathy from the strangers in whose house he now was, and his sobs subsided somewhat when Mama spoke to him quietly. But when the doctor came and began his work, Papa's cries became unbearable for me, so I looked for a door. Once I was outside, I walked away quickly so that I would hear no more of what was going on in the house.

I was soon watching a gaggle of geese at a water trough. A large gander must not have liked me so near. He flapped his huge wings, then stretched his long neck towards me. With his tongue and throat, he was showing me where the loud squawk came from. With that show of strength, he came towards me. Now it was my turn to cry as I ran for the house with a big goose tugging at my pants. We both made it to the porch. I got the screen door open, but could not open the kitchen door. As long as the goose stayed on the porch, he held me captive between the screen and the door.

Neighbors had gone down to the little bridge and could tell that Papa must have been thrown against a cement form. That is what must have caused a jagged cut from his hairline down to his nose. He would carry that scar for the rest of his life. They also reported that Dan must have been spooked by the noisy rattle of heavy paper which workmen had left behind.

The stitching took quite a while. I had to hear the last of the stitches and could have counted them because Papa sounded off anew as each new stitch came in line. The cut was long and must have been painful, because repairs were being done without anesthetic. Papa thought it would heal better that way. He told us later that he had had teeth pulled by a barber with only a corkscrew. Late that afternoon we were given a ride home by the people who had taken care of Papa. It was my first ride in an automobile.

The top-buggy needed repairs too, as did the harness. But Dan was not invited back to his stall.

* * *

The wound on Papa's forehead healed well, but it was a long time before he went without a bandage. Because everyone, especially a country pastor, needed some method of transportation, a horse was a necessity unless one could afford one of those new automobiles. But the buggy was soon repaired and a quiet, well meaning but sad looking, tame horse was in Dan's stall. Things were looking up again. Even the name of the new horse was fitting, for it was called "Teddy."

Papa chose one of these days, when he no longer needed a bandage, to go to Grafton. He had friends there, such as the pastor and the depot agent. But when he had not come home when expected, the question for the children once again was "Wo ist der Papa?"

Because there was no answer, we drifted to the area in front of the church, from which one could see in all directions. The corner was known as the "Rock Creek Corner." Each one of us was hoping to spy Papa with Teddy first. The few cars that went by didn't excite us, although they were still quite rare. The drivers were strangers. But then, of all things to happen, one of these noisy cars slowed down and turned into our yard. We thought it must be company, but when we came nearer we all joined together in a great shout of surprise. It was our Papa who was there behind the steering wheel! After all of us had a chance to sit in the front seat and squeeze the balloon of the squawk horn, Papa said to Mama, "This horse won't run away."

Papa had gone to Grafton that day all right. But he spent most of his time learning how to operate an auto. The Grafton Motor Company sold him a brand new, sparkling black Ford Touring Car that day. It came with three doors, a shiny brass radiator and the latest equipment, electric magneto lights.

* * *

In those days, cars were of little use in the winter because tires with traction for snow had not yet been developed and in Northern Iowa there usually was plenty of snow. Although Teddy took us to school every day, something was not working right. There was too much room between Teddy and the buggy, so he could not stop the buggy from coasting into his hocks when he was asked to halt. Instead of a wild reaction in preparation for a run-away, Teddy would stop and stand still, except for the fear that made him quiver. Then the driver would have to come down, pat his withers and calm him with soft talk. After being led for a few steps by the bridle, he would proceed. But even after the wheels had been taken off the buggy and exchanged with sled runners, something still seemed not to fit. It was then that we noticed that good old Teddy was adjusting to the bad situation somewhat by cringing with expectancy and taking short, quick steps when he felt the slightest check on the reins.

We had no trouble on our daily trips to school: Johanna was a good driver at 13 years. But Papa did not like the situation. He knew that something was not right, but he did not know what to do to correct it. He came to the thought that it must be the frame of the buggy that had been damaged as a result of the runaway.

One afternoon, during the last week before Christmas vacation, we came home from school and saw, to our surprise, there in the back yard among the elderberry trees, a red sleigh! Really, it was like the picture in our song book! We didn't get to wonder alone very long because Mama, with joy and happiness showing in her face, was out of the house quickly to give us the good news. Papa had it brought over just this morning. It wasn't a new sled, but it had blue cloth cushions. It was just great. Mama was so glad to describe how warm we would all be, snuggled together with that big brown buffalo robe for a cover.

After watching a happy family from the window, Papa came out and joined us. A neighbor had been over that morning and had brought a string of bells for Teddy's harness. The man had told Papa about such things as adjusting the harness to fit another horse, and also such things as blinders for the bridle. Everything could be fixed now. While Papa was fastening the bells on Teddy's harness, he said that he had thanked the neighbor for all the information that he should have had a year ago.

The neighbor had brought the bells over as a Christmas present for Teddy, because he had heard Papa was going to get that sleigh.

The McMillan Barber Shop was the best newspaper in town for those of us who were regular visitors.

Some "breaking news" even originated there. More than one side of the story always received time. Only a death as announced at a funeral was not to be disputed.

THE SLED

On our way to the swimming hole northeast of town at the grade opening, where all of us boys learned to swim before we knew about swimming suits, we would often stroll through the town's public dump grounds, poking into the heaps of refuse, wondering what we might uncover. To a twelve-year-old this side trip became a walk through a fantastic labyrinth of discards and throw-aways, of worn-out toys and broken treasures. Among this rubbish the birds sang and wild flowers splashed color among weeds. Often at our approach, a mouse would scurry to its nest in a sun-bleached mattress or possibly in an overturned coal scuttle. Certain piles of broken bricks or shards became landmarks to us. For me, this place was a playground or even a park.

There were no automobile graveyards then, but mechanics were already hauling worn and replaced auto parts to the dump grounds. My favorite finds among these piles from the garages were the tops of touring cars because they included the curved hickory staves which had held up the stretched canvas. With some form of a strap they became our skis, but more often we used them as hockey sticks. Best of all, two of them would make ideal runners for a sled.

I had a good sled that my father had made for me, but my younger brother didn't have one. I knew he would not get a "Flyer" or a "Snow King" like so many of the other boys, but if my father could see those staves, I knew he would agree they could be used to make a fine sled.

It wasn't until the snowy winter came that I described this cache of auto top staves to my father. He readily proposed that if I could get the staves home, he would make a sled for my brother. It would be a good sled, a sled with iron runners. It would be the best sled in town. We would not say a word about it to my brother; in fact, we would keep it a secret. That sled would be his gift from das Christkind.

We would have to hurry for by now the days had already numbered into the month of December. That year, the weather turned miserably cold very early. In my eagerness I decided to get those staves the day after I had the talk with my father. And so, after coming home from school I took a pair of pliers and a hammer and set out for the dump ground with my sled. My father was not at home just then. Reminding myself of my agreement with him to keep our business a secret, I decided to tell nobody — not even my mother — about my planned trip. I was happy with my secret and the anticipation it aroused. As I pulled my sled along the side of the road, I amused myself watching the steamy clouds that my breath formed in the icy air and the rime it deposited on my coat collar.

Like everything else at this time of year, the summertime identifications in my wonderland lay covered with snow and the smells of autumn were frozen in the winds of below-zero temperatures. I did well to locate my special assembly of staves, but soon found that pliers were unmanageable while wearing mitts. I tried to hurry, but when it is four below zero, working on steam-pressed hickory staves and their metal connections with bare hands in the open air of the dump grounds causes one to begin muttering to himself. What I had to do would have been a job of sorts even in the summer, but now not even the warmth of my arm pits would stay the progression of the frost biting into my fingers. The snow and ice were almost too much, but somehow I managed to get the staves loose, got them fastened to my sled with wire and then was ready to start for home.

It was already past dark. With this load on the sled, pulling it was not easy, the more so because I had to keep flailing my hands together (or so I thought) to keep them alive. The distance of a bit more than a mile and a quarter became a miserable haul. In the darkness it became harder and harder to keep the staves wired to the sled so that they would not constantly slide off so easily, for by this time my hands had become practically numb. I crossed the railroad tracks and made it to Porter's corner, six blocks from home. Unable to stand the misery any longer, I began to cry.

When I reached home and had the staves safely hidden in the snow behind the gooseberry bush, I tried to wipe the tears with my mitts and found that they were frozen to my cheeks. I was standing in the back entry of our house in this condition when someone opened the kitchen door for me. Everyone in the house was gathered there and I heard the ominous greeting, "Where in the world have you been?" I looked in vain for my father for I knew I could not expose my trip to the dump grounds to this audience. The pain in my frozen fingers was beyond description and the tears blotted my vision. I was not able to unbutton my coat or to take off my overshoes. I was totally helpless but for crying. Holding my hands in cold water seemed to sharpen the stings of the frost bite, and so the torture continued. I could hear the irritated questioning of my mother at my refusal to disclose where I had been, but having withstood the pressure up to this point, I was certain I would not tell now. My mother finally gave up and simply admonished me by saying that we would wait until Father came home.

After my brother and the rest of the children had gone to bed, my father, who had been at a meeting, came home. Finally I could explain where I had been. With an occasional sob, I apologized to my mother for my disobedience, and with her understanding, she joined our conspiracy. On the following day, Father took charge of the staves and started building the sled while we were all in school.

The refusal to explain my absence to Mother and her severe scolding, my frozen fingers and the disturbance I made that night were soon forgotten and never mentioned again. The last reminder I was to have came several days later when I was able to peel a thin white layer of tissue from my fingers.

After the sled was finished, it seemed as though Christmas would never come. But das Christkind never fails, and so on Christmas Eve we children gathered in the kitchen, as was our custom, after we came home from the church program. This was the time when our parents would help das Christkind bring the decorated tree into the living room from its hiding place in their bedroom, and our gifts that came with it would be placed in a semi-circle around the tree. Then from the youngest to the oldest, we would cover our eyes while being led into the front room where each of us was placed behind his gifts. The anticipation and the wait were almost unbearable. Finally, we could lower our hands, and in that moment of rapture, we sang a verse from "Alle Jahre Wieder," but my brother was already in motion before we had finished. He had spied the sled against the wall and knew that it was his. I could do nothing but watch him. He was in ecstasy! It was a heavy sled. The runners were of strap-iron an inch wide and they were polished to a silver shine and to an icy smoothness. It was a better sled than mine. I heard my brother say "Thanks" to das Christkind.

My brother has retired and now lives in California. During a recent visit, in which we were reminiscing about our home and our parents, I made mention of the scene I created one evening when I came home late with frozen fingers and then refused to tell Mother where I had been. Erwin remembered the incident and reminded me that on occasion I had very often been stubborn and obstinate. Then he asked me, "Why, after all, why didn't you tell Mama where you had been?"

I thought about his question for a moment, wondering why he would ask it. Suddenly, out of the blue, it came to me. I said to him, "Didn't you ever find out what happened the night I thought I was going to lose my fingers? I had gone to the dump to get the staves for your sled. Had I told everything that night, what would have become of your Christmas? Didn't we believe in das Christkind?"

SHATTERED HOPES

The water of little Rock Creek flowed sluggishly under the two bridges at the crossroads less than a quarter mile from the Mitchell County country school in north central Iowa. It was here that my public education began. Beside one of the bridges there was a deep pool which extended across the fence into the field. Sometimes men would come to fish there. The men most always had very large mustaches and smoked large pipes which produced a sweet aroma as the blue smoke floated away in the breeze. They would sit at the side of the bridge with legs hanging over the edge. When a wagon passed over, their weight deadened the rattling rumble of the plank on which they sat. The noon hour gave us boys enough time to sometimes walk over there to watch.

On my first trip to the bridge to watch, I noticed a shiny pail which was partly in the water down below. I lost no time creeping down there to investigate. Because I could hear a lot of agitation and splashing of water in the pail, curiosity made me lift the cover of the pail just enough to allow a peek. At this slight touch, the cover flew up instantaneously with a loud, tinny rattle and then fell with a clatter on the rocks. In this split flash of time I found out what the shiny pail was all about. While I was still in this happy state of astonishment, I heard (almost too late) the rapid snorting and loud, heavy breathing it took for the man sitting above to get into motion toward me. In his downward charge he shouted in very plain German "Was machst du da, Boop? Ich komm und schneit dir beide Ohren ab!" ("What are you doing there, boy? I'm coming to cut both of your ears off!") And so it was that this great moment of wonderment suddenly turned into stark fright! At this point my reflexes for self-preservation must have taken over.

There wasn't room under the bridge to make a get-away to the other side, but before I knew it, I must have made it because all at once I became aware of myself up in the dust of the road with my bare legs moving me very rapidly in the direction of the school. Never had I been talked to like that before. I could imagine the worst and when I was safely back in my first grade seat with Carley, (one of a family of three newcomers to school who was part of the song we sang about them "Johnny on the spot, Sophie on the pot, Carley in the barley bin.") I was very uneasy for a long time. Every few seconds I would feel my ears.

I didn't say much about this experience to anyone. I believed that I had learned a lot about fishing, surely enough to allow me to think about going fishing myself. Although I had never really seen a fish hook, I imagined them to be nearly like a small safety pin which I could get from my mother. I bent this pin just a bit and then tied one end of a piece of white store string to it. The other end I tied to a stout length of willow. I found a cork that was suitable and put it into my pocket. I needed some worms and would get them as I passed the garden. The first worm that I found, I impaled on the pin immediately. The second worm I put into my pocket with the cork. In this fashion, and with happy steps, I was off and on my way to fish in the creek.

On this particular day, Pastor and Mrs. Knappe of Alta Vista were visiting with my parents. The fact that there was company in the house made it easier for me to slip away without permission.

The point in the creek to which I was heading was in the direction opposite to the school, only a half a mile from home. Here the channel had been dredged and the water was clear and very shallow. I thought that this would improve my chances very much, for I could even see the little fishlings and it was easy for me to dangle my pin and worm right down to them, lolling in the shade between the rocks.

After much standing and bending over the area of my hopes, I noticed a brown leech solidly fastened to my barefooted ankle. Something told me that the worm, which had been longer than the fish I was teasing, was somewhat out of proportion. I didn't need the cork at all and the willow stick was in my way most of the time. I finally removed the tattered fragments of the worm from the pin and exchanged it for the one from my pocket, which was still alive. The second worm wasn't any more attractive to anything in the water than the first one had been.

I knew now that I must give up without catching the fish with which I could have saved face against the indignity of being reprimanded for leaving the premises without permission. In a hurry now, but with plans for future fishing, I headed for home. I stopped to cache my equipment beside the big rock by the fence where our yard started. Only I knew that I was lacking the fish which I had planned to show.

Just then my mother's voice, calling me, came through the trees of the garden.

* * *

There was a time in the spring of that year when cottontails were about to take over the lettuce and peas and other leafy garden sprouts in Mother's garden. It got to be a very bad situation. By the time Papa would get there with the shotgun, our little gray friends had run for cover. (Papa had bought the gun soon after being married, when he found himself unable to kill a rooster with an ax. Coming out with the gun was merely an anti-rabbit gesture, for I'm sure he was happy that they had run away.)

I felt sorry for my mother and told her that I would help find a way to get rid of the rabbits. In fact, I would catch the little beasts alive. Hardly had I made my plan clear when I was being teased by the older sisters. They offered to help me by furnishing a supply of salt which I should drop on the tails of the rabbits. They claimed this would make the entire process of catching them much easier. Their evident lack of faith angered me and I scoffed at their aggravating humor. I would show them!

I knew exactly what I would do. I went to the woodshed and carefully selected one of the larger wooden boxes, one that was light and had a complete cover. When I was sure that no one could see me, I carried the box past the chicken yard and set it down just outside of the fence, with the open side (which had been the top) pointing in the direction from which I thought the rabbits would come from the trees and the brush beyond the lilacs. I was sure that they would have to pass this spot, The garden was not far away, and I could see it plainly, because I had placed the box on a slight rise.

Now all that was left to be done was to fasten a piece of string to the box cover and leave it partially suspended just outside and in front of the lettuce which I had placed inside the box. The plan was simple; I would let go of the string at the very moment the rabbit hopped into the box for his feast. The cover would drop and the cottontail would be locked in the trap. I would know just when to drop the cover because I would be just behind the box and crouched so that the cottontail could not see me. (If I could describe all of this a little better, I would really have had a trap).

After everything had been set up, ready to go, there was nothing left to do but to wait for the first rabbit.

It was the rabbits themselves that showed me that something in my method was flawed. After at least an hour of expecting and hoping, I spotted, to my dismay, a happy little cottontail merrily hopping about in Mother's lettuce where he was making his lunch as usual. And he had not come near my checkpoint at all!

Suddenly I felt very tired and my legs ached from being in a cramped position for so long. I was unhappy because of the disillusionment and I thought it best to forget this whole adventure very quickly. To avoid further derision, I tossed the leafy greens from my catching-box and carried it back to the woodshed, where it would not suggest or call to mind further questions concerning my encounter with the cottontails.

Just then I heard my mother call.

* * *

That summer, Papa was paying a penny for every fifty flies we could kill with a fly swatter anywhere in the house. After seeing a large fly trap at Hartwig's Grocery store in St. Ansgar, I had visions of killing 50 flies more easily than with the swatter. Again, I went to the woodshed where this time I would make a fly trap for myself.

In the woodshed there were various lengths and scraps of wood pieces. There were also many kinds of large and small, bent and rusty nails scattered about in the debris that covered the earth floor. I even found pieces of used screen. After I had gathered the items I thought I needed, I got a hammer from Papa's shop. I knew what the trap should look like, but I didn't know much about different kinds of wood nor what nails to use.

Making the trap wasn't any trouble. Trouble, I thought, came from the hammer, for it seemed to hit my left thumb as though on purpose. And so it was that tears were soon making it hard for me to see. The flies, that I would be catching in a short while, were hovering over every part of my body that my sleeveless shirt and knee breeches left uncovered. I had to move every second to keep them from settling down to bite.

After some time I had to stand up. To clear my right leg of flies, I did a fast stomp-step like I had seen horses do, but chips and scraps and shards of many kinds were hard on the soles of my bare feet. I stood back and appraised my project before me. No one would guess that it could become a fly trap! I had not yet learned any fitting or proper curses, but I must have given vent to some cry of anger. Without any further decision now, quite in a frenzy, I turned to the corner behind me where the long handled ax stood against the wall. Had it been twice as heavy, it would have made little difference. I raised that ax with both hands and with two great heaves, I demolished my fly trap.

Then I returned the ax to its place and carried the hammer back to the shop. The wreckage I left marked the spot where my hopes of the day had collapsed. I didn't want to see it again.

This is when I heard Mother calling.

THE TRUANTS

A gnarly, old, weather-beaten door with several coats of peeling paint is hard on bare knuckles, especially when the temperature is below freezing. But after several hard raps one mid-December morning, I saw a movement of the window curtain. Then I heard steps. After that there was a loud, solid clank at the top of the door, as though an iron bolt had been released. This was followed by identical sounds coming from the bottom of the door. Then I heard a key clink in the latch, the knob was turned and the door opened.

"Good morning," I said "Are you Mrs Paine?"

"Yes," said the woman facing me. She was wearing a light blue housecoat with a colored, red poinsettia pinned near the left shoulder. Her feet, which barely protruded from under the long robe, were covered with blue slippers. Her skin was butternut brown and her dark eyes sparkled eloquently from settings in an attractive face. Her hair was done up in bundles, with several inches of loose ends hanging over her ears.

"I'm sorry about the door," she said. "Even though Christmas is coming on, you have to keep the doors locked, especially when you have children." Then she added with a smile "Come in."

"Ah, yes, thank you," I replied. "It is about the children I have come. I believe you have four. Are they here?"

"I imagine you are from the school," said Mrs. Paine.

"Yes. I am the Attendance Officer. I came to check on the children."

"They are here," said Mrs. Paine. Then she called loudly to the left. "Children, come out here." As if by magic, two boys and two girls, all neatly dressed, entered from a side room. From the tallest to the shortest, they stood erect and in a straight line, smiling at their mother and me.

"Children," said Mrs. Paine. "Show this man why you are not in school this morning." At that order, each child raised the right foot, removed the shoe and while still standing on the other leg, they showed me that they were without stockings.

"You see, that is why the children are not in school," she said. Then the children were told to go back to their room to play. The mother explained to me that all of the stockings had been washed and were hanging over the front room register to dry. While telling me about the hardships of a single mother raising a family of four children, she showed me the bathtub which she used to wash clothes because they had no washer. I suggested that some way could be found to locate used appliances for her. "Goodwill gave me a $10 certificate once," she responded. "The authorities come out and look, make promises of this and that, but I never hear from them again."

Back in the front room, I noticed several inspirational type song books and a Bible on the dining room table. "Someone must do some singing in this house," I commented, whereupon Mrs. Paine replied with a flourish, "Yes, indeed we sing. I always sing to my children. Would you like to hear me?" Resting on an arm of the davenport, I replied "Why certainly."

Mrs. Paine placed a record on the phonograph, then selected a song from one of the song books. Then she called her children in "To hear me sing for this man." They came and stood in line as before while she sang four or five verses accompanied by the record. When she had finished, she turned to her children and me with a happy smile. I commented that "It is nice to have a mother who can sing like that," and asked Mrs. Paine, "Do they ever sing to you in return?" A positive reply from her came very quickly, along with an invitation to hear them perform. "Thank you," I said. "I bet this will be good."

My visit by this time had become quite informal, almost cordial. For the singing, the children were given instructions by name: Daniel, the older boy and the older girl, Ruth, helped Michael and

Debra to properly cross their legs for sitting on the floor to sing. Daniel distributed the books after which his mother made a selection. She sounded the "key" and the chorus began. The first song had a revival tune. The words that I could make out concerned themselves with a prayer for love and mercy. Symbolic gestures gave life to the music. The second number was "Away in a Manger." I was quite taken in with their rendition of this old favorite. I clapped my hands and told them, "You will be able to enjoy singing all the rest of your lives."

Once more the children were sent to their room. Mrs. Paine informed me that her children were getting well acquainted with the Bible. "They will be strong Witnesses some day," she said. I asked her whether the children attended Sunday School. "I am a 'Jehovah's Witness'," she replied. "We do things our way. Would you like to hear them recite?"

Once more the call went out to the children; "Come in here and recite for this man." While they stood erect and in line, Mrs. Paine opened the Bible "at random" she said and started reading from the Prophet Daniel about "Shining Wisdom." Then she turned to a short reading from Revelation about burning candles. At certain places during the readings, she would stop and say "Blank," at which point the children would fill in a word in unison. "Did you notice the eagerness with which the responses came?" asked Mrs. Paine. I replied, "The recitation and everything else has been very impressive indeed."

After the children had been sent back to their room, I asked Mrs. Paine about their father and was told that "He would never be a good Witness" so it was just as well that he was stationed in Hawaii with the Army. Further information came quite rapidly, but it no longer fitted into the purpose of my professional visit. I wanted to know from what locality they had come to live in this town and was told, "We have lived in Washington and Florida and just about everywhere else. We do not like it here, especially the principal and the teachers. My first husband was no good. He had too many sex hang-ups, sort of like a pervert."

Finally, coming back to the business of my visit, I was assured that the children would be back in school as soon as their stockings were dry. I told her that I appreciated the time she had given me and suggested that she have her children learn the first and last verse of Psalm 103. Then I shouted a "Merry Christmas" into the house for the children. With a last reminder to Mrs. Paine to send her children to school because it was the law, I wished her a Merry Christmas. Then we said Good-bye to each other.

* * *

That afternoon, Mrs. Paine walked to the school with her children. There she berated the principal and accused him of allowing many obscenities to be taught to her children in the classroom. She was especially offended by the sex perversions which, she claimed, her boys were learning there.

However, she had kinder words for "the man" who had been sent to her home that morning, saying, "Now that was a nice man."

* * *

A week later I was notified of probable repeat truancy of the Paine boys and girls and was asked to verify the report. After I had filed my first report, a follow-up of the case had made me aware of Mrs. Paine's visit to the school and the comments she had made there about me. Remembering the cordial visit I had had with her, the high marks she had given me in the principal's office, and with Christmas only four days away, I was in high spirits as I approached the Paine's door. Even so, I felt a little bit guilty for hoping that I would not need to listen again to a recital such as the one presented on my last visit.

An inch of fresh snow sparkled in the morning sun and gave life to an otherwise quiet neighborhood.

After rapping hard several times, I again heard the door bolt at the top of the door moved, then the one at the bottom. A clink of the key removed the last obstacle to opening the door. By taking a few steps back, Mrs. Paine made it possible for me to cross the threshold and to close the door. She wanted to know immediately what my purpose was.

"I have come because of the children," I said. "I have a report that they are not in school today."

"No, they are not in school," she admitted. "I'm a good mother, and I could not send them because they don't have proper shoes. Come here, children, and show the man your shoes."

As on my previous visit, the children appeared as if by magic. Because I had not been invited into the house, we were still in the outer hall. There wasn't room for a straight line, but somehow, they all raised their right foot and showed me that they were wearing tennis shoes.

"I would be considered a bad mother if I were to send my children to school through this snow in those shoes," said Mrs. Paine.

"Those are the kind of shoes almost all the kids are wearing," I replied. "They give all the protection that is needed to get to school."

"I know best what my children need to wear," she argued.

"Those shoes look like they are nearly new and very sturdy," I said. Then I added "I'm sure that they would do very well."

"No one needs to advise me nor my children about what they are to wear," Mrs. Paine snapped. I could see a bit of fire in her eyes as she asked, "Why are you harassing me?"

"I'm not harassing you, Mrs. Paine," I explained. "I'm only interested in getting your boys and girls to school."

The children were peering eagerly from behind their mother's housecoat. After I added, "I am only doing my duty as Attendance Officer," she responded with an emotional outburst of censure, using choice words of street level language while cursing me soundly! Very angry now, she told me, "You have nothing to do with me. I know the law as well as you do."

I was shocked, scarcely able to believe that this tirade of vituperation was real! I finally broke in to remind her that "I thought you to be a Christian woman, so why do you curse me?"

Her voice was shrill and biting now as she replied," I curse you as a Christian. Now get out of my house."

Hurriedly, I put together a swift, "Please see that your children get to school so you can avoid having to go to court." Then I asked once more, "Why do you curse me?"

"Get out of the house, you----" followed by very abusive language and bad names. Those names were the last thing I heard her say after I had bidden the five Paines a very Merry Christmas. With one last glance at the four young ones, I succeeded in backing out through the door by which I had left so happily only a few days ago.

After the door closed behind me, I rolled my eyes toward Heaven and walked to my car. I was a bit unnerved and shaken by the beating I had taken. The clean white snow was refreshing. I quickly gathered my wits and reminded myself that there were only a few days left before Christmas. That thought put me back on track.

I turned one last time to look back to where I had been. The snow glistened as beautifully around the Paine house as around any house in the neighborhood.

> *For men and boys, the main piece of everyday clothing was the overall. Blue denim was usual for all ages. We combined pants and shirt into the "unionall" which was closed with buttons. Soon the zipper was invented, and used in place of buttons. This was the only piece of clothing boys would have to wear in the summer. We called them Jiffy suits.*

HARRY AND THE NATIONAL ANTHEM

The boy came to my class at mid-year. Because he was new, he was given Seat Number 1 in Row Number 1. This position was about five feet in front and to the right of where I quite often sat on the table in front of the room while conducting my classes when I was not on my feet.

Harry was dressed like other boys except that much of his clothing did not fit well. The rips and the worn places never seemed to get patched. Washing and laundering did not come often. His right shoe exposed a big toe which even a stocking did not cover. But Harry was always very quick to respond to any need that I or any nearby student might have such as picking up a dropped pencil or getting a book from the shelf or running an errand. And it was always "excuse me" when he had forgotten that one of his feet was in the aisle. Harry was never loud and he never showed anger. He was always present and never tardy. When Harry came into his seat, his brown eyes sparkled with a smile of greeting while he combed his dark tousled hair with the rough fingers of his right hand.

Judged by the results of the methods we use to rate, grade and classify our students, Harry did not have a chance. He could hardly write a complete simple sentence and his speech was just as troubled. Harry had no visible friends, but his classmates never abused him with adolescent ridicule. They must have respected him. He was just "Harry" to everyone.

Because Harry came in at mid-year, I had no references concerning his home conditions. In May Harry became an absentee for three successive days. I had a brief talk with my principal about this and he told me to drive out and find him. The address he gave me took me to one of the bunk houses that were left on the Air Base site in the northwest area of town at the close of World War II. The building with a number that matched the address I was looking for had an open porch with the west and the north sides boarded against the wind. Over it all there was a roof. An elderly gray-haired woman with several missing teeth sat on a bench behind a table on the porch. With her was an older man who left as I approached. A bottle on the table was empty.

Standing just below the steps, among the early green sprouts of weeds and grass and some of the past winter's debris of cans and blown paper, I asked "Could you please tell me, does a 'Harry' live here?" To that question the woman responded with, "Who are you?" After explaining who I was, I was directed by her pointed thumb to the rear of the building. Following her direction I cautiously proceeded into a darkening tunnel-like hallway where the square windows were still covered with heavy pink paper which had been put there for protection again the winds of the past winter. And there, in the semi-darkness, in the back corner on a top bunk, I found Harry. I reached up to touch him as I greeted him. He was happy to see me, and told me that his side was hurting him. But he promised that in a few days, he would be back in his seat at school.

That spring, at the end of the school year, I had to make out the usual reports which were needed for the office records. Among my many students, Harry, of course, was one that stood out from the others. But he needed a record too. When I came to his name I had to stop and think for a while. In the space for "comments" I crossed out "Civics" and replaced it with "Citizenship." And in the grade column for Harry, I put an "A."

One afternoon during the next winter, when I needed an extra copy of the daily newspaper, I stopped at the 'Argus' corner on Minnesota Avenue, and there was Harry at his usual spot with his canvas bag of papers. The temperature was about seven degrees below zero, but he greeted me with the same smile that I had known him by during the years before. We exchanged a paper for a coin, and then he waved me off with a "Thank you, Mr. Reinecke." Some years later while I was taking a Newspaper Class on a field trip through the Argus-Leader plant, I learned that Harry was working there as a helper to the oiler on the big press. After that I lost track of Harry. However, I am sure that Harry is busy somewhere and that he is happy, quietly doing someone a favor with a dependable service of some kind.

※ ※ ※

During the past November, one of the places we visited while driving through some of the eastern coast states was Charleston, South Carolina. From a vantage point, we could see Fort Sumter which stood guard in the harbor protecting the city. That Fort, of course, was captured early by the South, and so while mentally reviewing history a bit, I was taken back nearly 50 years to Fort McHenry, a fort which stood fast against the British while it protected the city of Baltimore in the War of 1812.

And then I imagined myself once more doing those annual lessons concerning our National Anthem and the conditions under which the Star-Spangled Banner was written. I rethought the times I would be on my feet, chalking diagrams on the blackboard, how I could describe and tell and show with my hands and voice in every way possible for me, how an American lawyer got caught on a British ship while he was arranging for the exchange of a prisoner of war and how he had to live through the crossfire of bombs and rockets that night while hunkering behind the balustrades of the boat he was on. Everyone was anxiously awaiting the next flare put up by soldiers of the fort which would show the flag still flying after the British fled in withdrawal.

At this moment I could not help but think of Harry once more. My classes were studies in citizenship and patriotism, and so when we came to the National Anthem and the flag as a symbol, my assignment always was for everyone to learn as many verses of the Star-Spangled Banner as possible, but learning the first verse was a requirement for everyone. After a week or ten days, the students were asked to write as much and as many verses as they had learned. Many had learned the four verses and wrote them totally without error.

This is what Harry wrote:

Oh, say, can you see
Buy the dawns early light
Was so gallantly proud, hailed
Twas the twilight, lasting, gleaming
Over the mountains and oceans
And home of the brave.

Oh say, can you hear?
Through all the guns and cannons
That they were still fighting
For the free and the home
To bring an end to it
So that there could be Peace.

Oh say! can you see
Through the fog and hear?
Through the gun and canons
And the soldiers yell
That they were still fighting?

Oh say, can you see?
By the dawns early
That the flag was still there
All torn
And burned
And shot up!
That we have won the war!

Oh, say, can you see
By the dawns early light
Over the home of the free
And the land of the brave.

In this vivid description of what transpired that night, we are reminded even in this "All torn, And burned And shot up" world of the wish and the longing of our hearts for Peace.

Harry did not have the right rhyme, but he did have the right reason. And he had an imagination equal to or greater than that of Francis Scott Key.

> *Every farmer kept at least eighteen milk cows. After the evening milking, they were let out by the older and most frugal farmer, and kept in a small corral for several hours and then turned back into the pasture. From time to time, some straw would be spread around the corral to be pressed as binder into the rising pile of manure which by fall had become ten to twelve inches deep. At this time, the cows were herded to a second corral and the first one was left to dry. When it had dried sufficiently, it could be spaded into pieces three or four inches thick. The sun would dry these bricks in a few days. At that time, they would be transferred to a place near the house and stacked near the kitchen door. This was fuel for the kitchen cook stove.*

FEEDING THE BIRDS

When the leaves have finished falling from the ash tree in the back yard, the table and the lawn chairs have been folded and stored under the porch and the Thanksgiving weekend has already slipped past, then Christmas is not far away. Those signs of the season remind me that it is once again time to hang the bird feeders among the bare branches and to refurnish the play area for the birds where a short time ago there was shade.

There are feeders with large openings for the bigger birds, such as the cardinals that like sunflower seeds, although they also feed on saffron seeds which they pull from the chickadee feeder. Another feeder, one with tiny holes, is filled with delicate black thistle seed. The finches talk and fight around that feeder until they turn golden in the spring. One of the feeders hangs from the roof just a few inches from our south window and because it is filled with a mixture of feed, it attracts all kinds of birds. They offer us a choice seat in our study of their society. We vie with the neighbor across the street as to which yard is visited by the most exotics. We observe how Mr. Cardinal finds a choice bit of food. After picking it up, he happily struts to his mate and graciously drops the morsel into her opened beak. Or we watch the chickadee on a branch with a saffron seed held firmly between his toes, as with triphammer speed he pounds the shell until it cracks and drops away, and he swallows the remaining heart. During the past summer an albino sparrow became a special member of our local bird commune.

Quite a number of years ago, when I first became interested in the needs of birds, I found that feeding them in the winter is a necessity, and all the more so when the ground is covered with snow. The food especially helps the weaker ones who would otherwise more easily become prey to severe weather and fall frozen to the ground.

One morning in the middle of December, when I was out filling the feeders, my next door neighbor happened to be out, too. Helene remarked that she was glad I had put the feeders out again, because she enjoyed watching the antics of the birds from her kitchen window. I responded by saying "The news of the feeders does not spread so fast among the birds when the weather is as comfortable as it is this year, and so I have been able to attract mostly just sparrows so far."

Helene looked at me for a moment and then said, "Who told you that you need not feed the sparrows?"

✳ ✳ ✳

They lived in the east end of town — a father, a mother, two girls and a boy. One scarcely ever saw the mother, who took in washing from some of the townspeople so that she might have a bit of cash in the house when her children needed a nickel or a dime at school. The father was a free-lance laborer who was known to be the best chimney builder in the county. When he built a chimney, it came out straight except at times when he expected a bottle to help him. The children, who were several years younger than I, seemed always to be fighting a runny nose. Although their clothes were patched and worn from wear, they were always clean.

We knew the family only as a 'poor family,' and heard about them only through visitors who came to our house. I didn't get to know the father until later, and then I felt sorry that I was among the boys who teased him for walking so clumsily. Those were the first remembrances I have of him. Sometimes, in such a condition, when he had already been oversupplied by his bootlegger, he would give a sixth grader half a dollar with which to buy him a 35¢ bottle of vanilla extract. He would proudly add, "and keep the change."

This kind of transaction usually was the prelude to too much external evidence of his unstable condition. Then the policeman would take him by the arm and instead of taking him home, he was led to the little square brick building behind the courthouse with iron bars across the small windows.

One cold day, late in the afternoon, my mother called me into the kitchen where she had a cardboard box the size of a canned fruit carton on the table. Mother had packed that box with a hot dish and other food to make a whole meal for that family. She told me to take the box over to their house right away before the food got cold.

I was to go there? What if someone saw me? I'm to go to a strange house inhabited by people who don't even belong to our church, and most likely don't go to church at all! Very reluctantly, I did as my mother told me. The box fitted well on my sled and I made up my mind to hurry and get this job over with, this errand of bringing supper to a family whose father was in jail.

The door opened to a steamy, smelly kitchen. A faint light hung from the ceiling. I took little note of what else was in the room because my eyes were attracted to the mother who appeared much different than I had expected. She had a loving, kindly face and she began to cry when I set the box on a chair and repeated what my mother had told me to say. "This is from my mother." She said I should tell you 'Merry Christmas'." Then I turned around and hurried out, glad that it was over.

I could not have been in that house even a minute, but the more I thought about what had transpired during the last few moments, the shorter the walk home became. I was warm all over when I reached our house and eager to talk to my mother.

I don't remember any of the details of our conversation, but she repeated several times, "Poor people. They get hungry, too."

A DOG IN COURT

Vatch and Bello were names of dogs we had at home when I was very young and I have had kind feelings toward all dogs ever since. So I can not forget the story of Jumper and Ruffy who, for a time at least, were two very much talked about dogs in the community in which I lived when I was about twelve years old.

The story started in mid-summer of the year when Martha announced that she would give each of her two boys one of the pups from Flossie's spring litter. One of the boys was her son and the other was her son-in-law. There was hardly a noticeable difference in the markings of the pups. Both were black with a white tuft under the chin. There were no registration formalities for either one, of course, and there was no clue as to which neighborhood friend of Flossie had paid her the visit. Martha, however, developed a strong feeling for the one she had named Ruffy and knew down deep that she would give him to her son, Herman. Jumper she would give to Jake.

The families of both boys, the Buehners and the Mahlhaffs, had been prosperous neighbors since Homesteading days. Both were able to give each son a quarter of land on which to stake his future. Farm buildings and modest homes were soon erected. Now they lived less than two miles from each other and less than a mile from Martha, who had assumed leadership in the Buehner family at the death of her husband.

After one of the dogs was found dead in the ditch beside the road, the loving relationship changed. Was it Jumper or was it Ruffy that had been hit? So now there was strife; life became bitter between these friendly neighbors because neither one could find proof with which to stake a good claim to the surviving dog.

By late fall of that year, it was evident that something else would have to be done. There had been enough of family meetings that had settled nothing. In just a short time the dogs had become such good companions and were so much at home on either farm that the dog now surviving and alone did not reveal with his behavior which of the two places was his real home.

Martha finally concluded that she must take matters into her own hands. She went to the neighboring city to the east and engaged the services of a Railroad Attorney, for it was well known by everyone that railroad lawyers were most proficient in any legal matter. Things would be straightened out by him, and of course, in her favor. But no sooner had she made her plan public then the Mahlhaff family went to the city in the opposite direction and secured the help of the top lawyer in that part of the state. He would certainly present the entire matter in proper perspective, which would favor her.

Both parties asked for an early settlement if possible, and the Court set December 18 as date for the trial. Exhibits, such as pictures, rope leashes, a diary, a large grain sack and a horse blanket, were turned over to the bailiff to be presented to the court as need for them arose during the trial. On the day before the trial, the surviving dog was put under the protection of the bailiff to assure the dog's presence at the conclusion of the trial, because it had been rumored that someone was going to do away with him as the surest way of settling the squabble.

That evening Judge Buntz visited the county jail and made a personal inspection of the dog. Since it was quartered in one of the cells, a regular prisoner's ration of hamburger and gravied potatoes was ordered for him. After the feeding, the bailiff and the judge examined the dog's teeth and stroked his head and neck. They decided that, as mongrels go, this one was an exceptionally worthy example. The judge ordered food and water to be brought at regular times during the length of the trial.

This case would be lively, to say the least. News about it had spread to neighboring and distant parts. People were filling the town early on that morning, December 18. Relatives, friends and the curious were busy in the cafes and stores and especially the halls of the Court House which buzzed with gossip and speculation. The weather looked upon the whole affair with favor and so there was constant milling about. But there was an air of importance about it all, especially since Martha had been overheard saying early that morning in the shoe department of the Corner Variety Store "Und wenns mir auch nu 500 dolar kost, mein Herman griegt den Hund." ("Even if it costs me $500, my Herman is going to get the dog.")

The people in the crowded courtroom rose at the entry of Judge Buntz. Strong odors of robust farmer perspiration and pungent waves of heady garlic were soon absorbed in anticipation of the coming action. The battle lines were soon visible. Gone was the talk of love of only a half year ago when the dogs were a gift. Any sorrow for the dog found dead by the roadside was now being consumed by the flames of jealousy and the hatred of acrimonious accusations.

The attorneys soon seemed to be at a loss as to just what method of persuasion to use to sway a popular decision. Nor did the judge seem to be satisfied with the proceeding in his court. He recessed the trial in early afternoon, hopeful that more substantial presentations would allow an early conclusion of the trial on the next day.

Then the judge called the two attorneys to his chambers for a short meeting at which time he told them that with the evidence thus far on record, and with little more to expect, it seemed unreasonable for them to ask him to decide which of the dogs had been killed, or which of the dogs had survived. The judge declared it to be a matter of the heart.

The question really should be "What is best for the surviving dog?"

If only the dog could talk! But the mongrel remained silent, even though he received another good meal that evening.

By the morning of the second day, the crowd became even larger than the one of the day before. The courtroom ran its overflow into the halls and down the stairs into the lower corridors. Only by hearsay did news from above filter down and out to the streets.

And so the court came to order for the second day. After three loud raps of the gavel, Judge Buntz announced in a serious tone as follows: "It would please the court if this case could be settled by the dog himself. I would therefore like to suggest, since the season of Christmas is so near, that we might all take the opportunity here to show our own spirit of the season. By all, I mean both parties here in my court, their counsel and all witnesses. May I suggest further that the dog, the center of all this controversy, be brought into this courtroom here before me, from his cell in the county jail immediately. As soon as this can be done, I will give the litigants opportunity to freely communicate with the dog in any way desired. Whoever is successful in persuading the dog to come to him, I will declare to be the rightful owner immediately."

Absolute silence fell over the courtroom. Those to whom the judge had directed his remarks came to a quick agreement. The bailiff was seen leaving the jail with the dog and apprehension was at a peak everywhere in the town. An ordinary farm and country mongrel in the county courtroom! A dog to be his own witness and exhibit at his own trial! A dog to be sentenced! Who would have believed it?

The dog was led up the first step towards the witness chair on the platform. After Judge Buntz had repeated his last instructions, he ordered the bailiff to release the dog from his leash. And now, in the area where the attorneys had jockeyed for favor, stood those for whom they had tried their best in proper decorum. Suddenly, as though on signal, there arose loud shouts of "Here Ruffy," and "Come, Jumper." There was begging, pleading, whistling, shouts of "Commeer" and much slapping of thighs. The performance brought tears to the eyes of some, but most of the spectators could not believe what they were seeing and hearing.

The dog seemed unperturbed by the noise for a few seconds, but as the din and confusion rose, he was seen to shrug his shoulders and lower his head and tail. Turning his back on the noisy crowd, the dog climbed the step up the platform. Using a low, crouching crawl, he immediately disappeared behind the Judge's bench.

By now all eyes were on Judge Buntz. He seemed to be looking down on his left side. His left arm was moving as though he was patting or stroking something. The dog had come to him and was now resting a white tufted chin on his lap!

With a great smile, still stroking the dog, Judge Buntz announced in a happy voice, "What a beautiful Christmas present!" With his right hand he grasped the gavel and rapped it sharply. "Case dismissed!"

There was a great "stock market crash" in the 1920's after the good years following the World War. Most people were unable to understand the economics, but both of the local banks in town were forced to close because neither one could produce enough cash to pay people who wanted to withdraw from their savings account. I could not pay for my football sweater nor my senior ring because my father could no longer write a check. The school paid for my letter, "L" for Leola, and for my captain's star. Later in the summer, when money became available, I paid for my sweater.

ANNIVERSARY

The end of November and the beginning of December is always a gala time for my wife, Alma, and me, primarily because we were married during that period and also because Thanksgiving Day and my birthday always show up close to each other on the calendar. Taking care of activities connected with those events sometimes makes us tardy in our preparations for Christmas. In 1981, we had the pleasure of celebrating our 40th wedding anniversary. Being married for 40 years put Alma and me in a typed minority of a kind. For us, at that stage of life, self-inquiry and retrospection were a rewarding therapy during our preparations. Recalling some of the near forgotten happenings of that summer forty years ago made for very enjoyable moments.

Although Alma and I met each other while both of us were teaching during the 1930's, we only became well acquainted with each other after I moved to Illinois and we began a voluminous exchange of letters. This form of courtship was quite inexpensive since it was possible to send a lot of love in an ounce of mail for three cents. I am sure that each of us spent at least five dollars on stamps during the years just prior to 1941. Sometimes the letters were overweight and sometimes we even sent them airmail.

In 1941, I had been in Moline for several years. That summer, Alma came to Moline, too. I was employed there in a Division of John Deere. Her intentions were to work there during the summer and return to school in Aberdeen in the fall. She immediately found work in a dress shop.

All was sunshine that summer. If there was a cloud, Alma and I were on it. The few months floated by on billows of love. Before we were aware of it, we had given each other the basic promises that usually lead to marriage. Humorous innuendo concerning arrangements for such an important event in our lives turned to sobering thought the more we realized the permanence of its consequence. Our planning weeks were happy weeks, most likely because neither of us had previous experience in these matters. We agreed that Thanksgiving Day would be an appropriate date and our pastor assured us that he could make arrangements for us in his schedule at five o'clock that afternoon.

Having the common sense of a small town boy, I knew that I would need clothes and accordingly stood for measurements for a suit. Besides the license and rings, there was little else that I thought needful to bother about. Alma, on the other hand, took a much more sophisticated approach to these matters of which I was just becoming aware. My bride-to-be supplied a feminine touch to the development of the formalities about which we would soon make public announcement. She even arranged for flowers which she said were necessary for the occasion.

We were not to see each other on our wedding day until the chimes in the parsonage clock tolled five. My car was hidden from those who might abuse it on such a day. Walking the 16 blocks to a happening of such importance, with a bit of ice and snow underfoot, wearing a pair of shoes that had not yet gotten used to my feet, still remains an incomparable lifetime experience.

Besides the two witnesses who would sign the document which made our wishes legal, my sister and her husband, and my brother and his wife were the only people to witness the rituals first-hand. Our best friends, who had been married just a month earlier, watched as much as they could of the ceremony by taking turns looking through an open space between the lowered window shade and the sill, while standing in the snow between the bushes next to the house. And so they knew that Alma had cried during the ceremony.

Now it was done! It was over! Alma and I were married!

After our party of four had eaten a Thanksgiving Dinner at a classy restaurant, where I enjoyed a bear steak, Alma and I went to retrieve our car. All we needed to do before leaving for Chicago was to pick up our packed bags which were ready at my rooming house. There we found the street full of parked cars and the house full to overflowing with friends. Mary and Joe, God bless them, the Polish people from whom I had rented my upstairs room for several years, had the dining room spread in the full fashion of a 100% Bohemian wedding.

This unplanned wedding celebration, the first of the many that would follow, did not change our plans concerning Chicago. So at about eleven o'clock we took our leave and were on our way. But before we left the outskirts of town, Alma and I made a stop at a little place we knew would have music and we would be alone. Too late we realized that almost two hours had slipped by, and there was no time to start on a trip to Chicago. We decided that my house would be well quieted down by this time and we would be able to smuggle ourselves up the stairs and into my room without detection. We also said, "What if! and So what!" because we were planning on living there until our apartment was ready in January anyway. But what a surprise we had when we got into the room! On the table, beside a vase of flowers, was a lighted and twinkling candle. Mary and Joe knew us pretty well. They knew we would be back.

Next morning, on our way to Chicago, we bought 35 cents worth of apples at a roadside stand.

* * *

Since that wedding, Alma and I have observed each anniversary in some way or another. After the 25th, every five years became more precious than the previous five. To commemorate the 40th, we simply said "It's our 40th" as justification for any excess or celebration beginning in early fall. And so we enjoyed "On Golden Pond" in Minneapolis and a Bear – Redskins game in Chicago. But we know that there is a deeper sense to life than just plays and games. Because our three children had been unable to attend our wedding, among other reasons, we decided it would be good to review and reaffirm our vows before them and other immediate relatives. Our pastor gladly took charge and made provisions for a proper ceremony in the little chapel. Years of time had prepared all of us for a better understanding of the depth of such abstractions as love, trust, honor and promise, than we had of such subjects during our unseasoned years. This time it was our daughters who cried. Tears were prevalent among the guests. Alma and I seemed to have stood the test of time.

After this half hour ceremony, we were delighted to continue the celebration in the form of a reception in the adjacent church parlors. Where 40 years ago even friends had stood outside, this event brought to us a couple who certainly were strangers to us, but who insisted that we must be related to their friends with the same name in Holstein, Iowa, so they too celebrated. It was a great afternoon of punch, cake, coffee, biscuits, nuts, congratulations, flowers, fellowship, new clothes, happiness and the mix of many, many people. Just as it had been fun 40 years ago, without experience, so it was fun this time. Alma and I learned that what we didn't know then hadn't hurt us in the meantime.

* * *

One day, while driving to Lake Poinsett with Alma, I was reminiscing about the events of the past forty years when my mind suddenly came upon a segment that needed clarification. I asked Alma, "How did it come about that you didn't go back to Aberdeen to finish school after that summer in Moline?" It took Alma a few seconds to get her mind out of the book she was reading. Then, in a matter of fact voice, she replied, "I certainly would have liked going back but when that thought came up, you simply said 'Alma, we're either going to get married, or let's forget all about it.' Remember?"

I choked a bit at her reply, and don't remember my immediate response. Of all the times I've put my foot down, I was glad to be reminded that that was one of them.

THE IRON

When fall stays on as late as it did this year (1979) one doesn't have the usual amount of time to get ready for Christmas. It always takes me several weeks just for the thinking, planning and preparation, not to mention the appropriations. And it reminds me of another Christmas when the weather was about as mild as it has been this year.

That year we had Pearl Harbor; this year we have Iran. That year Alma and I were married on Thanksgiving Day; this year we look at pictures of four grandchildren. That year our worldly possessions would have fitted neatly in a trunk; this year we are sorting and disposing of some of the accumulated mementos of the past 38 years.

In those days, single men did not live in apartments so I had a fine second floor sleeping room. For $12.50 per month I enjoyed my sun porch, a walk-in closet and an oak parlor table with a lamp on it by the window. Alma and I would live there until our apartment was ready for us in January. We both were working, we were extremely happy and surely believed that these were the best days of our lives.

In late afternoon on Christmas Eve of that year I was glad when I got home for I had carried Alma's present all the way from work downtown. It was quite heavy. The gift was wrapped in appropriate paper and tied with a red ribbon, and I proudly put it beside the little tree on our table. There already was a beautiful little package with a card which at a glance indicated that it was for me. My eyes must have sparkled at that moment of sheer joy and happiness. Alma and I threw our arms around one another and proclaimed our first Christmas together! A tree, gifts, a lovely wife — what more could I want or wish for? We went out to eat, then came back to celebrate Christmas Eve.

Our steps became lighter and lighter as we sang old carols together as we walked toward Third Street A. Our room was warm and everything was beautiful. Nothing had ever seemed so bright to me before. Finally came the moment for which I could hardly wait. Alma would open her present from me!

"This is my first Christmas present from you," she said. With eagerness and anticipation, Alma turned the package around several times in the process of unwrapping it. (I was always good at wrapping.) Suddenly I noticed the happiness in her face change to bewilderment and despair. Abandoning all restrain, my wife broke into sobs. The tears came in torrents. Her head was on my shoulder (I was wearing my tailor-made wedding suit) and the package was in her hands.

I had no experience in handling a case such as the one I now had on my hands. I did not know how to act and I was equally awkward at knowing what to do. Even if there was something wrong with my present, there was no possibility of exchange and no chance for correction or apology at that moment.

After placing the orange and black box with the electric iron back on the table, Alma sat down on the bed and cried some more. I could not understand it at all. Something must be wrong, that I knew. Could it be she had suddenly taken ill! But between her sobs and my futile attempts to comfort her, I heard Alma say quite plainly, though very plaintively, "If it had only been a little bottle of perfume, but an iron! Oh, no!"

That iron was used for many years, remaining a constant reminder of the lesson it taught me. Some time later, my Dad's only comment was, "You should have known better." The only happy memories of that iron was the day it refused to cooperate and had to be replaced.

As I said earlier, this year Alma and I are going through the rummage which takes up space and gathers dust in the basement. There, unmindful of what I had come upon, I found three irons tucked away, one of them still in the original box. I called Alma over and said "These irons ought to be taken to the fire stations where firemen repair them if possible and give them to a needy family." In a flash of remembrance that made her move quickly, Alma pointed at the orange and black box and said in tender reflection, "Oh, no, not that one! That was my first Christmas present from you."

We looked at each other for a second. Then we put our heads on each other's shoulders while we quietly and happily relived a once sad moment.

> My family thought everyone ought to be a member of some religious group. In the areas that were settled basically by Germans, the Catholics and the Lutherans predominated. There were groups called sects, consisting of people who had broken away from the mother Protestant church. It was in those early times that my dad wrote a thesis in the form of a 64 page book entitled "Church Unity." He thought ethnic groups should not be separated and didn't like the fact that the Lutherans settled individually and conducted services as they had done in the home country.

THE RAG FAMILY
AN ALLEGORY

Once upon a time a very poor family lived in an old railroad company house by the tracks in the west end of town. The father had lost his life while on duty for the company. As a matter of compensation, the railroad people had provided a house for his family to live in. The house had seen better days. Even though shingles were missing from the roof and pieces of siding were loose or gone entirely, even though a porch had dropped from some of its moorings and seemed ready to topple, trees and hardy flowers grew tall all around it among the weeds. The sweet smell of lilac drifted with the wind in the spring. This place had become the home of the Rag family; for Mother Rag, her son Calvin and her two daughters, Gloria and Liz.

As soon as all the children were old enough to attend school, it was easier for Mother Rag to do housework for folks in town. It was hard enough for her to buy sufficient, simple food with the money she had, to say nothing of clothes. What clothes they had, they wore again and again. The garments were washed over and over, until small worn places became holes. The knees were most vulnerable and soon became frayed and frazzled. The girls wore the dresses that someone would leave on the doorsteps. Mother Rag would do the needed alteration to make them fit. But jeans for Calvin were always too big, as were the suspenders and shoes. So it was that the three children, like their mother, never had anything else to wear except clothes that were already worn out when they were new to them.

In the evenings Mother Rag would sing or tell stories with her children. There was reading and homework to be done, and games to be played. Calvin kept a watchful eye over his sisters at school during the day, lest someone hurt them with a snide remark. They all learned to love and care for one another. Mother Rag would often cry when she watched her three children walk off to school looking so bedraggled, especially Calvin because his jeans were so tattered that they would be turned into shorts as soon as the weather got a little warmer towards spring.

The children of Mother Rag grew strong and remained healthy. Because they were dependable, the girls often got to do family chores for neighbors or sat for young ones. Calvin was happy to take over a large paper route. One morning when he was half through making his deliveries, he saw a flicker of yellow flame come from the window of the mayor's house. Dropping his papers, he rushed up to the front steps. He shouted and pounded until the glass in the door broke. He entered just in time to help a pair of coughing and half conscious people to safety. But just as he thought there was no time to lose and he must follow them outside, he heard the unmistakable cry of a child. Calvin's senses blurred as he turned his face against the acrid smoke. Then he heard the cry again! Only when Calvin had leaped from the back porch did he realize that he was holding a crying baby in his arms. The firemen and the police were there now and a TV crew arrived just in time to get good pictures of Calvin handing the baby to his hysterical mother. That picture of the Rag Family boy in his ragged, worn and patched clothes was seen on TV screens all over town. And there was more. The newspaper Calvin carried on his route the next day showed a large picture of the Rag Family boy as a young hero. Newsmen had come to talk with Calvin, but he had left the scene quickly because he could not explain how he found the baby, or how he got out of the house. He picked up the remaining papers and finished his deliveries.

At school the next day there was a great welcome as there always is for a real hero. Students liked the picture and they looked up to Calvin in childish awe. They wished that their jeans looked washed and worn, but they found that frayed and frazzled jeans do not happen overnight. So self-inflicted rips and cuts were showing up in the clothes that both boys and girls were wearing. Out-sized, loose clothing and big tennies with large, untied shoe-strings were the things to wear. And so it was that Calvin and his sisters, the Rag Family children, did not look out of place at all in the Christmas program at the school that year.

Eventually, elementary and high school years were finished. Their excellent achievements throughout those twelve years gave Calvin and his sisters an outstanding student status. Calvin had steady training at the bank and was ready to choose from scholarships offered by several schools. The girls also found places in good schools that would prepare them for a business career.

So it was that the Rag children all found work in the field for which they had prepared themselves. The girls very quickly got into the designing and merchandising of student clothes, while Calvin was busily climbing the ladder of a banking career. He even invested in some of the clothing ventures that were offered to him through his sisters. But they did not forget their mother. They had her well taken care of in a moderate condominium which they had built just recently, in the exact area near the tracks in the west side where once their childhood home had been.

In the meantime, the craze for washed-out and worn looking clothes had spread throughout the country. Store shelves were loaded with a variety of imitations. Boys and girls were now wearing the only style of clothes that the Rag Family ever owned. But Calvin was now married with a son of his own. Because he had worn enough of those ragged clothes years ago, Calvin didn't approve of the styles, much to the chagrin of his boy, socially conscious Young Cal.

* * *

Once again it was Christmas time. Mother Rag had become Gramma Rag. She was sitting alone in her comfortable living room, happy in knowing that her presents for her children and grandchildren had been delivered. Gramma Rag let her mind wander through her unforgettable past. She smiled once in a while and wiped a tear from her cheek as both the sad and happy events fled across her memory. She thought especially about her grandchild, Young Cal. Gramma Rag knew that for the Christmas Program this year he wanted most of all to be dressed like the others who sang in the musical number in which he had a part. Young Cal did not want to be the only one to wear dress pants and a white shirt. What she did not know was that Young Cal's mother had softened at the last minute and had purchased a washed-out pair of jeans for him to wear, even if only for this one occasion. Nor did anyone know that he had already borrowed additions to complement them.

Suddenly Gramma Rag got up. She went to a closet and rummaged through a trunk of old clothes. Finally she came out with what she was looking for, a pair of jeans. Much wear and many washings had given this garment a rich texture that could not be duplicated by acid vats and commercial tumblers. Gramma Rag had preserved as a treasure these jeans that her son Calvin had worn many years ago. Now she folded them neatly and, with a tender blessing, she wrapped them and had them delivered to Cal's house addressed to Young Cal with a note in an envelope. "Dear Young Cal: These are some jeans I thought you would enjoy wearing at the program tonight. Gramma."

That evening the Calvin Rag family made ready to go to the Christmas program. Mother and Dad Rag would pick up Gramma, while Young Cal chose to walk with a friend. "Hi there, Cal," said his friend, Sid. "That is a keen outfit you are in tonight!"

"Where did you get it?" asked his classmate, Nick. "Look at those hang-over suspenders, and those oversize two-color tennies with the draggy strings!"

Young Cal was given a rating of "ten" for his rags that evening. Some friends showed signs of envy, which made Young Cal very happy.

The audience filled the auditorium to capacity. A signal was given and the beginning number was announced. The curtain parted and from the wings came the members of the boys' chorus. Young Cal was among them. Tall and straight he stood as he assumed his place in the front row. Like the others, he scanned the crowd during the prelude. There, not far from the stage lights, sat his people, the Rags: Gramma Rag, his Mother Rag and his Father Rag. It took but a short glance to detect the displeasure in the eyes of his father. A quick glance at his mother convinced Cal that she was entirely bewildered and near consternation at what she saw. But when Young Cal's glance rested on Gramma, he caught a bright sparkle and a gleam coming from her eyes and noted that her face was radiant with happiness. Seeing that made Young Cal very happy, because he was certain she would help to mitigate difficulties that might arise with his parents concerning his clothes. And he sang as he had never sung before. Young Cal knew that he must be the happiest boy in the entire chorus. But he did not know that Gramma Rag was the happiest person in the entire auditorium because she knew whose jeans he was wearing.

> *Two magazines that came into our house every week were the Literary Digest and the Pathfinder. There were others, but I liked the Pathfinder for the advertisements that appealed to me, like those of selling Colliers magazine every week and earning two cents apiece, or selling twelve packs of garden seeds and getting a bag of twenty-five snotagate marbles. I especially liked the cartoons in the Literary Digest. For a long time I believed I would become a cartoonist.*

VATCH, MIETZE AND A GOOSE

There he stood on the platform above the noisy, smelly, smoking pit of the La Salle Street Station, among the crushing crowd of hurrying humanity. His left hand and wrist were wrapped in white cloth and his arm was cradled in a sling. He had just arrived on a train. Of the passing crowd, he addressed a kind-looking lady who he thought would help. With his German accent he spoke the words he had rehearsed, "Please help me find the Louis Pasteur Institute." The lady made no response. She turned away and was soon lost in the continuous surge of passing people. Then he took a step towards others and made the same approach, "Help." After some time, a man who heard the call came out from the crowd, grasped him by his free arm, and personally conducted him to the Pasteur Institute.

That is how Papa got to the Institute. He had been badly bitten by a vicious rabid dog as he was entering a gate to visit one of his parishioners. Only by raising an arm in time was he able to protect his face and throat for which the dog was lunging. It was only recently that Pasteur had discovered an anti-rabies vaccine in his laboratory in Paris, and the nearest supply of that vaccine was in the Chicago Institute.

The whole experience of having been bitten by a dog that had to be destroyed because it was found to be rabid did not change Papa's love for dogs. During mid-December, in a visit with the local doctor, he was assured that the vaccine had done its work well and left no side effects. This alone was happy news, and it alone would clear the stars for Christmas. But friends had found a quiet little brown pup which they thought would be a suitable gift for their pastor at that time. And they were right. He and the pup were immediate friends. Papa had never had a dog of his own before. He named him Vatch.

Little Vatch remained with the family until I was two or three years old. I don't remember anything about Vatch except his fight with two other dogs which Mama and I saw and heard from the front room window. That was the last day of his life. When Papa came home that noon and saw that Vatch was hurt beyond hope, he picked the dog up and carried him away. It was a sad day. And because he could not bear to have this happen again, Papa decided he could not have another dog. And he never did.

* * *

She sat there quietly in her wheelchair, with a tablet and pen on her lap, watching the glittering decorations and the lights on the Christmas tree. The cat came into the room and had his eyes on the tree also. He had learned that Mama in that wheel chair left him to prowl about anywhere with impunity. The lower tinsel was easy prey for cat play and Mama thought she could control things with a scaring "ssss" now and then. But she became uneasy thinking that the cat might cause the tree to topple as he began going for the higher prizes. It was during one of the upward maneuvers that Mama gathered enough strength to noisily shuffle her slippers, raise her hands as best she could and then shout emphatically "Kaatz!" At that moment, the cat came down with a string of lights clasped in his claws. But with one or two leaps of surprise and fright, he was halfway up the winding stairs, going to where he had never gone before while Mama was looking. And all she could say to him now was "Well, go ahead and go!"

Mama, of course, had her own ideas about house pets. She grew up on a farm where cats and dogs were kept in the barn, but since cats were also kept in homes for the control of mice, there was always a cat in our house. Whether they were male or female, I remember only one by name, "Mietze." The rest were all just "kitty." It was Mama who saw to it that the cats were let in and out of the house at regular times and that they always had their food and water. The cats had a place in the corner behind the water reservoir of the kitchen stove. Even so, although she had no great love for cats, Mama always took care of their needs, even if it meant some medication for repeatedly frozen ear tips or a nipped nose.

When arthritis disabled Mama more and more, she had to give up her kitchen duties one after another. Then when she became confined to the wheelchair, she lost some of her zest and enjoyment of life. The episode between her and the cat in front of the Christmas tree was the last straw.

* * *

My older sister took care of the several dozen chickens we always kept in a fence. One spring she fooled a setting hen with four goose eggs, one of which hatched. The hen treated the offspring like a mother should, but the chickens took issue with this situation. A special pen had to be built for the goose to ensure its segregation and safety. But soon it was led outside of the chicken yard, and there it learned about special human attention from such friends of animals as Papa.

Papa would sit down on his haunches somewhere in the shade and the goose, which had grown and developed very well during the summer, would come to him because it had learned that there would be food in his hand. They would quabble and talk and quabble and talk with each other, sometimes for long stretches of time. Whenever Papa was in the yard, the goose was beside him; it was his security. It would sit patiently by the back porch steps. No stranger, not even friends, could come to the back door in safety. The goose would hiss and roar and beat its wings until someone opened the door from within.

We speculated on the gender of the goose and decided it was a gander because of its fierce actions and the raucous sound of his hissing aggressiveness towards others while protecting Papa. If Papa allowed it, and he did on several occasions, the goose would follow him up the steps and into the porch and on into the kitchen, always announcing himself with a loud blast on his trumpet. But he didn't negotiate all of the stairs to Papa's study. He would scream wildly and half fly for nearly two blocks toward town, while following Papa who was driving away from home in his one-door Model T Sedan.

Mama didn't mind the gander except when she was hanging out clothes. She had a clothes line on both sides of a cement walk. One day, when Mother had just filled both sides with sheets, the gander, having just exercised himself in a puddle, came strolling down the cement path towards her. All at once he noticed that he was practically locked in and must have lost his mind. He began to sound off and to flail the sheets with his wings, flying one way and then the other. When Mama saw what the goose had done to her sheets, her wish once more put his life in jeopardy. Just then a car stopped in front of the house and since no one was at home, Mama went to see who it was.

The visitors happened to be old friends from the country. It was a good time for Mama to rid herself of some goose trouble. She thought of how he wouldn't allow friends to visit, how he ran after the car like a dog, and all the other nuisances he made of himself. Even if we could butcher it, no one would eat him. He wasn't fit to keep, and so on and on.

We could not believe it when we found out that the goose was gone. Was he run over, or did someone come and haul him away? Maybe he followed the car too far. But he would come back. Everybody knew whose goose it was. Mama was the only person at home and she had nothing to say. We could not incriminate her, for she was our mother.

Before the year was up, a note arrived from out of town. All it said was "Thanks for the Christmas Goose!"

> *Many people did not like President Wilson because he lied to the people to be re-elected. They said in the campaign, "He kept us out of war, and he will keep us out of war." But shortly after the election, he declared war against Germany.*

WAITING FOR THE MAIL

The mail carrier of today is rapidly becoming an impersonal worker. The substance he brings to us is composed mostly of second and third class matter such as catalogs of the Miles Kimball, L. L. Bean and Spencer variety that tell us what we should buy, or the political brochures, of which we have had a great deal lately, that tell us what we should think and how we should vote. Gone are the carriers that occasionally sang or whistled while carrying their leather bags along their route. Yet, it was only thirty years ago that our Mr. Besco stopped long enough on the front steps to enjoy a cup of coffee and make a brief report concerning a good fishing trip of the previous week-end. It could have irritated the next householder on the route who may have been waiting for his mail, but on another day it might be his day for a personal call. But the steps of today's carrier are measured by the time-study people and there is no allowance made for friendly stops along the way.

By this time of the month, most of the seasonal advertising has been delivered. Now the first class letters with hand written addresses are appearing in great numbers. They are the signs of the Christmas messages we have been waiting for.

Seventy-five years ago, it was the custom of the people to gather in the General Store at Massbach, Illinois in the forenoon. Some of them took the opportunity to make a purchase of a needed grocery or notion. Others were just quietly listening to those who always knew the more intimate news of the community.

Some of the people were in lively discussion concerning the meaning and the merit of items carried in the Chicago Tribune. The blacksmith from across the street, the buttermaker from the creamery up the hill, and the preacher from the south end of the village were always interested participants. At this time of the year, just a bit more than a month since the election, Mr. Taft's victory was, in most people's opinion, a happy ending to the campaign.

What all of the people were really doing there in the store that morning, like all other mornings, was waiting for the mail.

Massbach was a tiny community in the southern part of Jo Daviess County of Illinois. It was a very hilly, but beautiful area that was settled by German immigrants. The government maintained a Post Office in the general store which was operated by partners Heid and Dittmar. Mr. Dittmar would have become Postmaster had Mr. Taft lost the election. These two partners were sure to keep the location of the post office in their store. One or the other of them would always be appointed Postmaster since one was a Democrat and the other a Republican. At the present time, of course, Mr. Heid, the Republican, was Postmaster. That might have been a directing omen concerning my own political affiliation in what, at that time, was the future.

Suddenly the noisy group became quiet. Overshoes and heavy clothes rustled and hands were raised to cup the ears. The purpose of the waiting once more became the prime interest because the long moan of the Great Western's steam whistle was heard as it echoed and re-echoed among the valleys and hills that frosty morning. Mr. Heid would have to cross a beginning finger of Terrapin Ridge and finish his trip to get the mail from the station by way of the Ridge Road that led into the village.

(It was this Ridge Road that my father had to go over with his horse and buggy to bring a doctor from Savanna when I was born early in December of that year. There was a cold, wet drizzle to contend with that night, and in the darkness he walked and led the horse because of the treacherous roadway. Possibly his position on foot was less precarious than that of the doctor who sat in the buggy with its scary jostling and sudden jerks caused by the deep ruts and the slippage in the grass of the uneven terrain. But the doctor had experience; he braced his feet against the dashboard and held on to the staves of the top. Otherwise he would have been pitched out of the buggy bodily, onto the wet and muddy countryside.)

After the last shrill whistle of the train had announced its departure from the area, it was only a short while until Mr. Heid appeared with the gray sacks of mail. Then it did not take long for Mr. Heid and Mr. Dittmar to channel all of the parcels to the proper cubby hole. At that moment, the big window was pushed up with a loud bang.

Because it was near Christmas time, there was quite a bit more mail than usual. As the packages were handed out through the window, one could recognize the inexpert wrapping, but one could also detect the personal touch of the Christmas giver who had sent them.

Those packages, letters and picture cards were the mail that the people of Massbach had waited for.

* * *

Seven years later, during the years of World War I, in a location roughly 200 miles west of the Mississippi River from Massbach, when we heard the sudden clattering rumble of Tabberts bridge, we would unconsciously stop everything for a moment, hoping to hear the more pleasant sound of the harness bells, signaling to us that it was noon and the mailman was coming. The sound of the horses and the wagon coming over the bridge was different from that made by Mr. Bublitz in his new Reo at 25 miles an hour, or that made by Emil Kroneman in his slow-moving Olds. When the weather was wet, the boards of the bridge sounded like a short roll of thunder, but no matter. The bells that identified with the horses and the coming of the mailman, were always the same. Their rhythm told us that our wait that noon for our mailman, Mr. Dougherty, had ended. He carried the mail for Rural Route Number 1, out of Mitchell, Iowa.

Our church and the parsonage were located on the southwest corner of the intersection of two dirt roads. That crossing was commonly known as the Rock Creek Corner, or more simply, just "the corner." On the other side of the road, the mailman maintained a shed, along with the other rest stops for horses at the corner, and there he would take a break at noon. He would unhitch his team, bring the sometimes sweaty horses into the shed, feed and water them and give them an hour of rest. During that time, he too would eat his lunch in the wagon.

The vehicle this mailman used to service his route, for which he had made a contract with the government, is hard to describe. His wagon can best be imagined by placing three refrigerator cartons vertically side by side, then cradling them on and between the axles of two sets of buggy wheels. Vehicles of this nature, painted in red, white and blue with the US Mail logo displayed proudly, and drawn by a good team of trotters was the typical means by which even the smallest outpost was kept in communication with the rest of the country.

Best of all it was free! One only paid to send something. That was the meaning of Rural Free Delivery or RFD. It was a bit of personal humor for my father that in his earliest time in this country the US MAIL on his mailbox should read OUR, for that was the proper grammar he had learned in Germany. He used this experience as an example to show us the importance of proper punctuation.

The standard model of our mailman's wagon compared very favorably with that of the Watkins Man or the coffee salesmen or even the fishmonger who all plied their wares throughout the countryside. The only difference was that inside the mailman's wagon there was a cubby hole for each family on the route. Certainly, the mailman was happy when he could weigh a package and apply the proper stamps, but primarily he served; he did not hawk his wares. The mailman would sell you a penny postcard and practically guarantee with his life that for that penny it would be safely delivered anywhere in the country. He was very proud of that.

Because the mailman spent at least an hour at our corner every day, my father spent quite a little time in conversation with him. This was good because it was an excellent way to improve his English. But it was a bad time because the fortunes of the war in Europe hung in the balance at times. My father had left his home country and had come to America only 14 years prior to the start of the war so he was aware of some of the misinformation and untruths that the newspapers were printing. For this reason Mr. Dougherty, of course, considered him pro-German. Some friends even went so far as to suspect the mailman of having had a hand in bringing my father's name to the attention of men like Mr. McNider and other politicians who had connections with the War Committees, and still others who worked as vigilantes.

One afternoon a delegation of three men was sent out to arrest my father who was at a meeting. The men brought him home, and in his study they interrogated him for an hour and a half.

When they ended their illegal inquest and their search among his files and papers without having given him the benefit of a witness, they picked up a few papers and mementos and prepared to leave, indicating to my father that he was coming with them. When they got to the door and saw the entire churchyard filled with farmers and neighbors of the area who had been alerted by the telephone grapevine to meet quickly at "the corner," they left in a hurry, but alone.

Mr. Dougherty was a personal friend to everyone on his route, even to my father. He knew where the aunts and the uncles lived. Letters with a black border he would deliver to the door of the house with his own added sympathy. Since he spent so much time regularly at our corner, we considered him as some sort of a neighbor with unwritten permission to use the premises. He would come to the back porch and pump water to carry to his horses. In the winter he brought along his flat stone footwarmer for my mother to reheat on the kitchen stove for him.

At Christmas time our mailman would observe the season by slipping on a Santa Claus mask, complete with the long white beard, over his head. With loud but merry shouts of "Merry Christmas," he would carry a package to the house, knowing full well that it was a Christmas present from a relative. He knew that our gifts would come from Ohio. My father did not fully appreciate this interpretation of the Spirit of Christmas. We were being taught to believe in das Christkind.

This visit by the mailman would repeat itself every day with only a slight variation. The need for a stamp was sometimes temporarily forgotten in the rush of just knowing that the mail had come.

When the mailman had tossed the reins over the dash and closed the door behind him, the fading song of the harness bells would tell us that the mailman had gone.

The wait for the mail to come another day would begin almost immediately.

Most people had two sets of clothes, one for every day and the other set for Sunday. All men had at least one dress pants and a white shirt. They were reserved for Sunday. Most boys had a set of Sunday pants and shirt, too. Any other clothing could be used during the week. The best was saved for church, but could be exchanged after dinner for older clothes.

A FALSE BOTTOM

The days of the Prohibition Era were benevolently referred to by my father as "The Noble Experiment." That period was the source for the plot of many stories and films which depict some of the many events that took place in the lives of people during those times.

During World War I my family lived in north-central Iowa, and during the great flu epidemic the song "It's a long Way to Tipperary," with which the soldiers had sung their way across to England, had been paraphrased to "It's a Long Way to Blooming Prairie," namely to the little town a hundred or so miles to the north in Minnesota. Those people had not yet voted themselves dry and it was possible still to get medicinal brandy there. My father was very happy when some of the neighbors brought back a large bottle of peppermint schnapps for him on their last trip there, especially since it arrived just before our whole family, except father, came down sick. He told us later that the few drops of schnapps in sweetened warm water he had given us on a spoon may just have been what saved our lives. It was said later that many lives were lost during the flu epidemic because the most common medicine used for such ailments as flu had been eliminated from the household shelves because of Prohibition.

The following year, my family moved to a little town in north-central South Dakota. I was in the Fifth Grade then. There was still much talk of the flu of the past year, and more so because now a flu-like epidemic was making the rounds of the hog feed lots inflicting heavy losses there. Those farmers who at that time had a large batch of mash brewing were fortunate if they mixed it with the ground feed they fed their pigs, for that seemed to save them. Others lost their entire herd. Prohibition made no reference to pigs, and a veterinarian was not available for advice in those years.

During the time of the "Roaring Twenties," when a large car like a Buick or Hupmobile came through town heading east in the dust of Highway 10, we would say "There goes a bootlegger," especially if the car was loaded down to the springs. It was rumored that there were brewing stills in the hills northwest of us.

Sometimes a local citizen or a stranger would give us boys a half dollar to buy a bottle of vanilla extract for them, and let us keep the 15¢ the storekeeper gave us in change. Those were in times when hooch was hard to find. My mother made me stop getting into that kind of business very quickly. And then there were the times when hobos would happily saunter down town in the summer evening after having nipped too much of a heavy drink. They entertained us by telling of their great deeds and we marveled at their wisdom. Occasionally, one of the residents of the jungle would assemble enough money to buy a little bottle of hooch from a bootlegger in town. One of them happened to come across a group of us youngsters in front of the drug store one evening. He persisted in showing us how to shoot "craps" on the sidewalk. The top of a bottle was peeking out of his hip pocket. It wasn't long before one of the boys pulled the bottle out of his pocket while the hobo was crouched on his knees demonstrating his skill. The hobo jumped up howling with rage. As the group of boys dispersed, he vowed that "I will be back with help and cut your bellies wide open." The street remained empty for the rest of the evening.

One of the same kind, on another evening, was more cooperative. As he half reclined on the steps of the bank on the corner in an open, sleepy stupor, one of us would tickle his neck or his ear with a dry fox tail. Then we would snicker at his quick reaction in slapping his back and shouting swear words at the "damn flies."

While in high school, neither I nor any of my friends ever consumed any kind of intoxicating liquor. The first real information we had about it was what we learned in chemistry class concerning the fermentation process which in the end produced alcohol.

We had learned that liquor was bad and that Prohibition was the law. In fact, we were told and many of us believed, that most of the rotgut was so strong that a fine spray of it would disintegrate the barb wire barricade that was set up at the border to keep bootleggers from bringing the stuff into the United States from the south.

The stories I have mentioned in brief are examples of provoking instances that I remember from those years. We youngsters were not asked to solve the great problem. Amendment 18 became unworkable and after fourteen years of futile existence, it was repealed.

But at this time of year there is one story of which a recent postage stamp reminded me. It depicts an Oil Wagon of the 1890's with horses as pull power. It was only thirty years later that motorized trucks were common, so the gasoline Bob was delivering that Monday morning after Thanksgiving had the latest equipment made for hauling liquid bulk. He was on his way to a farmer in Koto and whistled as he drove through the sparkling rays of sunshine that played over a road he had traveled hundreds of times. Bob knew the fence posts almost by number and name, and he knew which badger had worked hardest during the past night. While he was slowly viewing the rising flat toward the glacial moraine that we called "The Hills," he had come to Bartletts Grove, two miles north of town. No one lived within a half mile of the grove which consisted of scrub ash and a variety of weeds. Suddenly there was a blinding reflection coming from a patch of short sunflowers and brush sprouts just beyond the ditch of the road. This was something new, something startling, something that had not been there before. Bob slowed the truck to a stop and as he jumped from the cab, he became wary of the situation and approached the spot very cautiously. A bright gallon tin can had caused the reflection and he recognized it for what it was at once. Bob grew nervous and a bit afraid when he saw that he did not have to deal with one can, but with a large neatly stacked pile of dozens of cans. This was not the hidden cache of one man, but part of a big operation! Bending low, with a can under his arm, he hurried to his truck before a hidden guard could cause trouble.

At this point, Bob forgot about his delivery. With one last look at the spot and a scan of the entire countryside for any movement, he left the scene and drove back to town in a hurry. A jacket covered the can beside him. His closest friend, to whom he told his breath-taking story, would not have believed him had it not been for the gallon he had brought along as proof. A third friend was called and all agreed that this was not about a small operation. The driver of the load must have become aware of a double-cross and because that put his life in jeopardy he decided to ditch the hot stuff on the chance of picking it up again at a later date when the heat was off. The snowfall of the previous week had made a perfect cover, but the warm week-end uncovered it all.

Hurriedly, the sample of liquor in the can was given the usual three tests. First the finger test which showed how well a finger wet with alcohol cooled when the hand was waved; second the taste test, done with the tongue; last of all, the burn test in which a small amount of liquid was judged by its flame. The sample having passed all tests was judged to be of high quality.

These three friends were all considered to be high class citizens in the community and so it took a lot of courage for them to go about this daring venture. They pledged themselves to a unity of share and share alike in whatever might come to them in the pursuit of this risky business. With an oil company box-truck and a pickup, the three left town for their secret destination. Everything was just as Bob had told them. The truck was driven through the ditch right next to the cans and the pickup circled the area as lookout. In a few minutes all of nearly 200 cans were loaded. With hardly a word having been spoken, the pull-out was without a skid, and in minutes both vehicles were in the alley behind the Post Office. Each of the three chose a sample and walked through the dilapidated basement door. And now it was time to really sample it!

To the amazement and chagrin of each one in turn, they found that none of them could pour more than a small cup of alcohol out of their gallon can, yet their can was not empty! A pencil quickly found the false bottom! They had heard of such a thing, but they did not expect such foul play to happen to them! Their mood of disappointment lightened somewhat when they realized that even 200 cups is quite a quantity. And how noble it was for them to have saved all those suckers from spending $25 for one cupful of alcohol!

Nothing more was ever said about this happening. Some time later the papers carried a story saying "Recently a large consignment of liquor intended for interests in Chicago was lost to Federal Agents when it was hijacked somewhere between Mound City, South Dakota and Browns Valley, Minnesota. Value of the hijacked liquor is estimated at $5,000 and its diversion will limit the Christmas cheer at its intended destination."

In the basement of the building where once the McPherson County Herald was printed and the post office did business, there hung for many years a sample of a gallon can with a false bottom which was used by crooked bootleggers. The front of the can had been cut away and the false bottom in the form of a cone showed how it was soldered to the inside of the top of the can. The little blob of solder to the right was for the entry of the methanol cut, frost free water filler. Many years ago, this can was removed and it is said to be on exhibit somewhere in a Museum of Prohibition Memorabilia.

> "Count that day lost whose low descending sun views from your hand no worthy action done." That was a lesson Augusta Doescher wrote in my memory book when she was my third grade teacher.

GOOD SAMARITANS

Late in the Fall of 1996, Alma and I spent ten days with my sister in Michigan. We had not thought of snow that early in the year and we almost got caught in the snow while on a short side-trip into Ohio to see other relatives. We got out all right and in time, or we would have been stranded for a few days.

There had been much snow here too, but when we looked out of the front window the morning after getting home, we noticed that our walks were clean. I noticed definite tracks of a snowblower. I had not made arrangements with anyone to keep our walks clean in our absence. Who could have done this?

That afternoon my niece, Margaret, told me that the day before, when she came here to take in the mail and the paper, a man came by with a snowblower. He inquired of her when we would be home, then told her "Martin has gone by our house for many years with his snowblower. Now that I have a new one, I think it is time to do his." Then he added, "Tell him not to worry. I'll take care of it."

The good neighbor on the south side of our block had no idea of the length and severity of the four winter months ahead. But he said "I'll take care of it." And he did.

* * *

Several years ago there were people who saw a need for feeding those who had lost their work unexpectedly, or for any other reason temporarily had no money for a meal. Arrangements were made to use part of a St. Vincent De Paul building in the northern part of downtown Sioux Falls for this need. Under a supervisor, teams of volunteers were organized by such groups as churches, business places, clubs and other groups who would furnish the supplies and the workers to serve a meal one day at a time. Even teams from out of town applied to be assigned for a day of service.

A crowd of humanity has been gathering since before five o'clock that afternoon, waiting patiently for the side door to open. Because it is cold out in the alleyway to the door, a volunteer works his way through the people offering them a drink of hot cider.

At 5:30 all is ready inside. All tables are covered with a tablecloth and each table is decorated with a small vase of fresh flowers. The door is opened from the inside and now the chilly group comes in amid joy and happiness. All of them are hungry. Some of them have been here before, maybe often, and for some it is a new experience. There are the big and the burly, the kindly little people and the young ones, mothers guiding one or more toddlers and grandmothers taking care of others. Some need a cane, but even those in a wheelchair will go home happy. Most of them have something to talk about with their neighbor that brings out a smile or a cheery burst of laughter. Others are very much to themselves and alone.

In the line which they have formed while coming through the door, they move past the kitchen window and are served. If needed, a member of the team will help a guest getting plates to a table. Members of the team also take a place in the line at some time during the evening and eat with the guests. Some of the guests have said a private prayer, but they all say that this meal is the best they have had in a long, long time. Sometimes shoes and mittens, items of clothing and school supplies are distributed among the guests. There are no left-overs on any plate as they all bring their used utensils to the dropoff provided for them.

The earliest diners are slowly beginning to leave to make room for those still coming in. And so this scene repeats itself, night after night, night after night, except on Sunday. There may even be a lunch on Saturday. Teams must prepare for at least 350 for each evening. It was getting dark when this group gathered in the alley by the door. When they came in, they were not checked by the doorman. They were not asked for their name. They did not have to sign anything. They didn't even have a ticket. Now fed, thankful and cheered up, they reluctantly left, going their various ways into the night.

Now the table cloths will be taken up, tables and chairs cleaned and all chairs set on the tables. The floor will be mopped. The kitchen will be clean and ready for the team that will prepare the supper for the Banquet tomorrow.

* * *

Last week a 20-year-old truck driver rolled over on the Interstate about 20 miles north of Sioux Falls. His load of nearly 10,000 gallons of gasoline caught fire. The driver was pinned in the cab by the steering apparatus and could not free himself.

The first passing motorist that stopped found that the driver was still in the cab of the machine. He was able to get in to the truck driver, but he was unable to free him from the tight clasp the steering column had on the trucker. But he still stayed in the cab. By the time five fire trucks and other equipment arrived, the fire had gotten so hot that the front tires began to burn.

The story in the Argus Leader finished its report of the accident this way: "A passer-by who was among the first at the scene stayed in the truck with Winge (the 20-year-old truck driver) while the fire fighters tried to free him. The mystery man was able to help the Fire Captain hook a log chain to the steering wheel. After the fire fighters pulled the steering column off and freed Winge, the man disappeared into the night. 'The truck driver was brave. We had some brave help,' said the Fire Chief of the passer-by."

* * *

The people in these stories remind me of a line in a poem Longfellow wrote about 130 years ago.
"Christmas Bells"
"Then pealed the bells more loud and deep,
God is not dead, nor does He sleep."

I believe that human needs are fulfilled by other humans who believe in the Promise of Bethlehem. That is how God works.

> *Pneumatic tires were a great boon to the more extensive use of the car. But tires were not able to withstand rocks and nails that caused tires to go flat during a trip and required repairs on the spot. My dad did not like the ordinary foot pump that came with the car, so he bought a pump which could be clamped to the running board. It was faster and easier to operate. Dad soon had that pump as a permanent fixture on the foot step on the left side of the car. In the 1920's, the first Model T Ford sedans had only one door on the driver's side. At a filling station, the local blacksmith happened to notice the pump and asked, "Who drilled those holes on the slant through that iron?" When he was told that Dad did it himself, the blacksmith completed his job and advised my father that he should take up blacksmithing and make a little more money.*

THREE VIGNETTES

Win or Lose; It's a Tie

My family was told early one year that I could not think of a thing that I needed or wanted for Christmas. I had been well taken care of in the past years so I issued a special warning against buying me those $42 and up ties!

However, for our 50th Anniversary, I purchased a jacket and thought to myself that it really would look better with a new tie. How could I find an excuse now for a new tie without paying a price for all I had said?

Looking neither to the right nor to the left, I walked quickly down the aisle toward the Men's Department. Suddenly, directly to my left in the haberdashery, stood four tall trees of beautiful, lavishly colored four-in-hand ties! They were just the colors I was looking for. No one was there to see the gleam in my eyes as I chose one of those rainbow-beauty ties. It was marked at eight dollars and some cents. To myself I said, "I did it. No one will know where I got this tie."

The first time I wore it was to the open house for our Anniversary Fest. The tie got many high marks. Maybe they thought I had gotten one of those expensive pieces of painted silk. Looks really count!

The second time I wore it was to a festive Sunday morning worship. At the close of the service I rose and turned to the couple in the pew behind us. I immediately recognized the man. He was a good friend who is connected with a prestigious financial group. During our brief greeting, but before I had a chance to compliment him on his beautiful voice, he commended me on my choice of ties. I responded with a quick review of what I thought of those $42 ties, telling him that I had simply gone to K-Mart. Because he was wearing a bright new tie himself, I complimented him on it and jokingly added, "I'll bet you didn't get yours for eight dollars though." My friend smiled and said, "No, I didn't. I happened to be in New York two weeks ago. I bought it from a street vendor there for three dollars."

* * *

Any Port In a Storm

At 10:30 in the forenoon of St. Patricks Day in 1964, I had loaded my niece, Margaret Novak, and three other lady teachers in my car. Now we were ready to leave for a three day Classroom Teachers meeting, which was scheduled for Rochester, Minnesota. We were aware of a coming snowstorm, but thought we could stay ahead of it. At this time of year, past the middle of March, we thought it couldn't be so bad. But the storm struck early, it struck suddenly, and it struck very hard. We barely got to Beaver Creek, just 14 miles east of Sioux Falls. There, at a filling station, we were told to go back quickly or the roads would no longer remain open. We hurried, but did not make it up the ramp to the Interstate. We were stuck and could move in no direction.

I got out of the car to see whether a push would help, but the fierce wind blew me over and I fell into snow up to my hips. The whirling snow blinded my eyes and I could not breathe. In just a few seconds my clothes were completely blown full of snow. I had to get back into the car while I still could.

Big, heavy trucks can go through snow where a passenger car cannot. Several went by us. We did not see them, but we could hear them over the rage of the storm. I'm sure they didn't see us either. Finally a chicken truck almost collided with us and had to stop. He took two of the lady teachers in his cab. Luckily, a pickup truck loaded with $600 of hog serum, which had followed too closely, had to stop there too. Without waiting for an invitation, the two remaining lady teachers managed to get into the cab with that driver. How they did it I don't know. I had gotten out and picked my suit case from the trunk. I quickly threw it into the box with the serum and then pushed myself into the cab with the two teachers and the driver.

The front office of a filling station is not the best place to change a complete set of clothes, especially when they are soaked completely and one is shaking and shivering. A cup of coffee and a blanket helped, while my wet things were drying behind the heater.

By mid-afternoon nearly 40 people had taken sanctuary in "our" Phillips 66 station. A man in a large car did not accept the invitation to stay, nor did he heed the warning not to drive any farther. Instead, he haughtily drove away. A bit later a young man and his wife came into the station. Though snow-blown and tired, they were happy to have found shelter. The lady was very pregnant, so she was given the bedroom in the living quarters immediately. Darkness was settling in and there were no more arrivals.

We were realizing more and more just how lucky we were to be safe, taken in by the two kind people who operated the station. There was a five stool lunch counter connected to the station. We were invited to use anything we thought would help to relax our taut nerves. We called our friends at home to let them know that we were safe. The atmosphere seemed to make us comfortable and we felt at home. Some of us were drinking coffee or pop. On one side of a table a Rummy game was in progress, while on the other side it was Cribbage. There was singing and some napping. Even here, time was as busy as ever

Before we knew it, daylight was coming and with it the sun. The wind had gone down during the night, but so had the temperature. Everyone was awake and the mood was up and positive. There was bacon frying in the lunch room. Just then the cafe door opened and in stumbled a man, the same man who had refused to stay the night before. He managed to give his name and where he was from. But before he could reach a stool, the man crumpled together in a dead faint on the floor. We carried him to the davenport where the ladies took his shoes and socks off and began rubbing his legs and feet with little response from him.

At eight o'clock, we were reminded by the loud cry of a newborn baby of what had been happening on the other side of the wall from the man with the frozen feet. A welcome shout went up from the crowd. A mid-wife appeared suddenly from somewhere. The radio announced the road to Sioux Falls was open, one way. An Army bus that had stayed in town over-night stopped in for gas, and then was ready to drive on.

We five teachers had missed the meeting, but just maybe we could still get there. We decided to ride back home in the Army bus. I gave my keys to the station man who would see to it that my car got dug out. Now, once more, we were on our way to Rochester!

Home in Sioux Falls, we quickly packed a second set of clothes. Then via the airport and Minneapolis, we arrived at our destination late that afternoon. We had finally made it!

What we and others did at that meeting in the Kahler complex has been forgotten. However, what was learned from living through an overnight with a motley group of many wonderful strangers, hosted by Verlyn and Luetta Arp, the kind and gracious filling station operator and his wife, I will always remember.

(The Arps still live near that station. The boy that was born there now lives in the Pipestone area. We five teachers are all still living.)

* * *

Psalms My Mother Taught Me

No excuse was acceptable to my mother when, for example, I tracked fresh mud onto her kitchen floor, especially on a Saturday afternoon. She would not believe my story of "I didn't mean it" when I hit my brother with my homemade bow and arrow as he sat peacefully perched on the branch of a big maple tree. She knew when the chickens had not been fed and everyone could see that many times I had not washed my hands before I sat down at her supper table.

Those were the types of infractions (and certainly there were many others) in my social behavior and development over which she was entrusted guardianship. Mother had her way of doing things without a referral to Freud or to Skinner. In one case I was simply given a pail and a mop. In the other, it was just a matter of breaking the bow that had propelled the errant arrow.

However, Mother must have had, quite unknowingly, a subliminal purpose in mind through which she planned to replace the scrub brush or the broken bow with something a bit more refined. She loved poetry and received much inner satisfaction from verses and proverbs. So it was that one day, after an instance such as with the scrub pail, she introduced me to Psalm No. 1. Getting acquainted with it meant the Psalm was to be memorized! The future became foreboding when I learned that there were 149 more Psalms in the Good Book. I must have been near incorrigibility, for it wasn't long before I had memorized about ten percent of them. That is when she turned to the songs in the hymnal -a book that contained the words for 595 songs!

What I had learned in German for my mother had to be learned in English also, because that became part of my preparation for Confirmation. Luther's Small Catechism became the text. To most of the candidates that consisted of the Commandments, the Creed and the Lord's Prayer, with explanations. I found out during four summer sessions of five full weeks that there was much, much more to it. But by then, studying had become easier because my mother had taught me so much, especially how to memorize.

The mind does develop wonderful thoughts. When I was deep into the Psalms, I thought David lived far too long and spent too much time writing Psalms. Had I shared that thought with my mother, I'm sure I would have gotten acquainted with at least one more Psalm. When I finished with the 94th line of the 12 verses of Song No. 383, I wondered whether Paul Gerhardt was smiling when he looked down on me, because somehow I was getting hooked on all this memorization myself! For when I fed our cow, Blume, with her ration of hay, I would be reminded of "My own being of grass" as it says in Psalm 90 and again in Psalm 103. And when I looked northwestward, across the prairie to the glacial moraine, I was certain I was looking to the hills of Psalm 121.

But what would life be like today if I could not think of Blume when driving past a herd of cattle in a field eating grass? Or if I could not transpose myself into a part of a bale of hay as it flies past me in a truck?

Alma has often wondered how I happened to learn by heart such a number of Psalms and songs. I give credit for that to my mother. She thought it would be good for me, and that is all the reason she needed. I treasure every line that her memory cult had me memorize.

"Mach End O Herr, Mach Ende" (Make an end, Oh Lord, make an end) is what verse 12 of #383 begins with. I will make an end on that note too.

> *Big news and little news, national, state or local, was discussed during the day in the local barber shop. I didn't know it then, but I was learning a lot about human behavior just by listening. We boys didn't offer our thoughts until we were sure we had a viable story, High schoolers would often debate their issues in the barber shop. There was always more news in the two barber shops than in the newspaper or the Herald.*

TRUE GIFTS

Sometimes it becomes hard to explain just why we give, as well as what we give. Some people don't believe in giving at all, which is probably a throwback to tribal days when all gifts were regarded with suspicion. Our early ancestors may have been more outspoken than we are for in the background of early Germanic language the word "gift" was used to designate poison, and that word is still used that way in the German of today.

By now I may have reminded you of the story of Snow White and the apple given to her by the wicked Queen, and also of the story of Pandora. But I want to quickly tell you about three other stories.

One of them is about Lisa who had a tattered bag in which she always carried some of her possessions, even though its main use during the day was to carry her books and school supplies from room to room. Some of the kids poked fun at her peculiarities. She wore the same dress for weeks at a time. She didn't spend time in the halls gossiping. She just wasn't a sensation for anyone. On the morning of the last day of school before the Christmas holidays, she went from room to room and, with a smile that shone through her straggling hair, she reached into her dusty bag and brought out a frosted cookie, one for each of her teachers. Hers was the only treat brought to school that day. Unmindful of any activity or commotion about her, Lisa made sure that she didn't forget the bag that afternoon for, as usual, her little dog would sleep on it again that night.

Then there is the story Alma and I remember so well about our own Mary. After saving her first fifty hours of baby-sitting money, which she earned at the rate of twenty-five cents an hour, Mary blew it all in one short moment by making payment on a special order of fresh fruit which would later be delivered to her parents for Christmas.

And then there is the story about our nephew's eight year old son who is quite a ball player. After his team won the State Bantam League Championship there was an unfortunate confusion involving a miscount. When the medals to the members of the winning team were handed out, one of the boys did not receive one. The over-looked boy turned his head and in utter dejection burst into tears of despair accompanied by loud sobbing. On the way home from the tournament that day, my nephew asked his son to show him the medal he had won, but the little slugger could not produce it. Finally, he confessed that he had given it to the boy that was crying.

These three stories are examples of giving without any premeditated objectives or strings attached. But why were the gifts given? They were given because there was love and compassion in the giver. Those are the only ingredients of a true gift.

> *When I was 12 or 13 years old, I swept the lobby and the back floors of the Bank of Leola. I would get up at seven, walk three blocks to the back door of the bank for which I had the key. On rainy days, I would have to mop the tiled floor of the lobby. That wasn't so bad, but I hated to clean out the spittoon. Pay was 50¢ a day.*

ALL ABOARD

My father and I often had our most intimate and memorable talks late in the evening before going to bed, while sharing some dark rye with cheese and warmed over coffee. The great depression of the 1930's was a bad time and that night we were talking about the young folks striking out for California to find their fortune. Father told of a number of instances he remembered from his "Wander Years" when he was looking for work. As we talked, it became increasingly evident to him that Bob, my roommate at school, and I had speculated on making such a trip to California, too. Father commented only that "one learns a lot in travels like that." I was looking for a more definite negative or positive reaction concerning my plans and so I suggested with a bit of humor that "We could even look up that Dream Plot that Mama teases you about once in a while. You know, the land an agent sold you for your retirement place in Texas." At that, he moved. With a thoughtful turn of his head, my father said, "That would be something."

The next morning he was busy first with the Atlas, then with his little steel box with the padlock. Later he made ready a 2" by 2" piece of bond paper with the formal or legal description of the plot in question, hand-written, on it. Papa had also written the name and address of the man who sent him five dollars on the years when it rained and his cows had grazed across the area.

Two days later I said good-bye to my mother, to my youngest sister and to my father who squeezed a ten dollar bill into my hand. Then I left to meet Bob in Golden, Colorado. The years slip away as I remember that day. I am once again that young man embarking on an exciting journey into the unknown.

* * *

Bob is finishing his work at the School of Mines. We decide that hitch-hiking will be too slow if we want to stay together, so we opt to "go hobo" and ride the rails. We bundle two Indian blankets together with a little satchel containing an extra shirt, socks, shaving supplies and soap. We are off to Denver!

It is quite an experience to walk past the United States mint carrying a tramp's bundle. We are tempted to stop and ask for a job there, but we are too busy. We turn south and go down Colfax Avenue to the railroad tracks. The first contact we make is with a person we think is a seasoned hobo. He points to a stringer that is about to go south, so we keep our eye on that line. Several hobos go for a flat car, so we move with them. We need to learn some signals. This is our first ride, and it is on an open flat car. The Denver Rio Grande line is carrying us. Our first lesson is to shield our eyes from the soot and ash spray so we ride facing backwards. Sheer exhilaration!

Short stops allow us to get coffee and move into an open box car. It is already cold at Palmer Lake. There we are ordered out and into a melon car. After some switching, we are rolling south again with about fifteen others in our car. There is much swaying and bumping. Colorado Springs and Pueblo lie ahead. It is getting very cold.

At daybreak, everything comes to a halt. We run across the tracks for some hot coffee. Since we will ride all day, we buy rolls and bologna for the day's lunch. When we began to roll again, Bob feels sick. We are ordered into other cars several times during the switching of cars. We suspect those stops were shake-outs, since our group is getting smaller. We plan to make Amarillo late that evening, but it is late already. It is one o'clock in the morning when we finally arrive.

Bob and I have not yet learned that the bright side, the one with the depot, is for paying customers. The yard side, the dark side, is for us Hobos. But the lights of Amarillo are inviting. We proceed to a near-by Phillips 66 station and seem to be welcome when we ask to wash up. But before we can say "thank you" on the way out, we are led away by two security men. They inform us we are being taken to "care and quarter." But before we know it, they have taken us across the street to an eleventh floor Police Station!

In the next few minutes, we leave our finger prints, names, next of kin, year of birth, color of hair and eyes, and other data to fill in their records. For other identification, I thought it proper to show them my 2 inch square piece of paper. The authorities ask for an explanation, and carefully examine Bob's DeMolay card. They want to know what our business is here. Then we are led to a visiting room with two other hobos. Bob and I guess that this is a regular jail cell. We are in jail. We are left there to our own thoughts. Our thoughts are very quiet. We hear talk and snoring from cells adjacent to ours. It will soon be morning. Bob and I slouch together on a big wooden bench and share our bundle for a pillow.

At 8:30 AM we are taken to a room for chicory and a roll. After we get back, I am called to answer a telephone call. Bob cannot go with me. The call is from the Sheriff of the next county. It has to do with my identification. On my way back, I overhear someone say "Neither of them looks like the Houston rapist." Then comes more waiting. Next comes a thin lunch with chicory. At 4:00 PM Bob and I are called out together and led down the hall to the elevator. We feel freedom in the air. But the elevator goes down only three flights and we are led into a court room. We are stunned by the rote swiftness of the Judge's lecture. Bob and I are not ready to hear him say "Ten days. One day's grace for time you have already served."

One of the guards picks up our bundle and takes us back up to the eleventh floor office. Where will we be stored we wonder as we enter the elevator once more. But this time it doesn't stop until it comes to the street floor. There the guard tells us to take good care of our identity cards because they were good for us here. Then he points his finger to the tracks and tells us a southbound train will be leaving in half an hour. Bob and I give a curt but honest expression of "Thank you, Sir." We smile at each other at this turn of events. We are speechless for some time as we hustle off to the yards.

When we arrive, the string to which the guard has pointed us is already in motion. We need to grab the rod on the run. We do not want to stay in the space between the two cars just over the coupling, so at the first slow-down we go for the top. We know that there is a catwalk on the top of the box car. There is no safety in sitting there, but we cannot go back down at this speed. So we lie down, one on each side of the catwalk and hold on with one hand. The sway of the car is much more noticeable up here. It is a very dangerous ride for us. Nobody knows that we are up here. After about twenty minutes, we come to a stop. Bob and I can hardly loosen our grip, but quickly scramble down and find a safer place to ride and to rest.

We need to keep our eyes open for a slowdown or stop at Post. That is our signal, because the stop after that is as near to Vincent as we can get. And that, after all, is our destination. We arrive there at one o'clock in the morning. We are happy to see an open gas station, although it is another Phillips 66. But the man is friendly. We identify ourselves. He is interested in South Dakota, but says he would not live there because of rattlesnakes. Then he tells us of their tarantulas and warns us we don't want to get bitten by one. "But," he adds, "they seldom show up. I haven't seen a tarantula this summer." After a few quiet moments, he rises from the bench, hurries to the edge of the cement and stomps on a tarantula! "That's the first one I have seen in a long time," he says resuming his seat on the bench. Then he points to the park where we can sleep.

We miss his directions, but on the other side of a two-wire fence, we find a beautiful place to lie down. All talk and thought of tarantulas ends quickly as sleep takes over. We awaken long after sunrise. Horned toads are sharing our quarters with us. We have enjoyed a quiet night in a cow pasture.

The day man is on duty at the gas station. By the time we get there, he is waiting for us. He has the information we asked for and directs us to a grocery store opposite from the court house. The owner is an old timer. He and his wife live in the back room of the store. When Bob and I present ourselves, we are regarded quite skeptically, but he makes us feel comfortable. After a short conversation, our host goes to the back room and uses the telephone. Then he returns with his wife and introduces us to her. After leaving instructions with his wife, the man invites us to have dinner with them. While he is doing a few errands, we are left to wait on a bench in the front of the store. Before long he returns, and we four, complete strangers only hours ago, sit down to say grace and enjoy a great dinner. Bob and I are now in Snyder, Texas and about to get our first taste of okra.

Mr. and Mrs. Von Roeder are our host and hostess, the people with whom we are at table. While we are finishing the meal, our host announces that he has the pickup ready. We will go out and try to find the place I am looking for. There are two extra rifles on the rack which we will use to hunt jackrabbits on this trip. We drive for miles and miles in many directions, over flat countryside covered with mesquite and cactus. There are no roads here. Neither do we see any fences.

Finally the pick-up comes to a halt. I think Mr. Von Roeder has spied another rabbit, but he tells us to get out of the vehicle. We are near the signs of an arroyo with nothing else but wilderness in sight. Our host turns his head this way and that. Then, with a sniff of the air he says, "I am sure that somewhere, within a mile or two of this spot where we are standing, is the patch of ground that land agent sold to your Pappy." Silence is the only "Thank you" out here. I scratch the dirt with my fingers and wish I had a container in which to take some of it home. I can say no more than another "Thank you." This is what we came here to find.

While cleaning the rifles there is more conversation about our parents and the plans that Bob and I have. My host will tell the rancher whose cows graze the land we saw that I have been here. After many best wishes and thanks for their hospitality, Bob and I pick up our bundle and leave. We walk to the Phillips station. The afternoon freight is not always on time, but it always stops. We will be in El Paso by morning.

We have time to choose an open car and are greeted by a dozen others who are taking advantage of this D&RG southbound. There is a lot of worry and speculation among the men in the car concerning the treatment one can expect going west. We hear that hobos of all shades are treated as vagrants. We hear that at the California line all those who cannot produce seven dollars and fifty cents are put on the next car going east. This news is scary to us. Bob and I decide that we have accomplished the big purpose of the trip. We agree that we have had enough of the bulls in the yards and on the tracks and the police on the streets. We decide to return home. The promise to my father is completed. It is easier to think of going home than to think of going deeper into a strange land.

But now that we are in El Paso, we must take advantage of our nearness to Juarez and Old Mexico. We will cross the Rio Grande and at least get a taste of tequila and the ability to say "We even left the country." At the entry to the bridge that we are to return on there is a large staging area where many hundreds of people meet coming or going across the bridge. We are fascinated by the variations in dress and behavior and are engaged in watching. Not a word of English is to be heard, but a little eight or nine year old boy wearing only a pair of shorts comes to me and looks up into my eyes. Motioning to his shoe stand, he says "Dust shoes, three cents." I consider that cheap and say yes.

The boy backs me against the wall and I put my foot up. His partner appears and motions to my other foot. The first boy says "Polish?" and I reply "Sure, sure, polish good." Both boys are busy.

Then comes the call once more, "Shine?" and I say, "Sure, shine good." When they are done, I try to settle for three cents. "No! no!" they protest. "Each job three cents. Dusting, three cents. Polishing, three cents. Shining three cents for one shoe. Your two shoes now makes eighteen cents." Bob is getting the same treatment from a different pair of nice-looking, shiny, bareback boys engaged in a similar business.

So now, back to El Paso. The tracks are not far and we are lucky to find a string being made up to head north. The bulls do not bother us, they must know we are leaving. It's a slow ride lasting that afternoon and all night. There are a number of stops, but only one change of cars. Late that morning, the train stops in a very large railroad yard. We set out searching for something to eat. Everything is beautiful and people seem very friendly. We even find a YMCA. Bob and I are soon as cleaned up as we can be. We can even read the newspaper and check on the railroad timetables.

We are in Albuquerque, a great place to stop. But Bob thinks we are not moving fast enough. Passenger trains move faster and our finances tell us we better move faster, too! So we decide to go all out and ride the fastest train, the Santa Fe Chief, out of this town. The brochure states that the Chief is the most luxurious facility between Los Angeles and Chicago. It will come through here at dusk and make a very brief stop. We will ride the blinds. Our bundle is expressed to Golden, Colorado. Bob and I slowly walk across a block of tracks with others, believing we are unseen. The other side of the train will face the depot. That side is for paying customers.

It is getting dusk and the sun is gone. We are nervous. This is new to me. I sense that we are not alone. Are Bob and I getting into trouble? At least, we are together. It is dark now. The long, moving whine of the Chief can be heard coming toward us. In seconds it is just a block of tracks away. Suddenly lights come on and it is as bright as day. There, ahead of us, stops this giant monster. It is hissing and frothing and seems to be shaking and boiling. I feel that I must urinate, then find that I have peed already. At that moment, as if on signal, the area just ahead of us comes alive with many hobos scrambling across the tracks like ants. The scene is alive!

Most of the would-be riders are faster than Bob and I because they know what they are doing. Bob gets on ahead of me. He scrambles with the others to the flat top of the water reserve. I don't make it and must hang on tight to the grab bar of the tender with one hand, but I do have a foot on the step. By this time, we are pulling out of the station. I am between the engine tender and the first express car, just above the coupling. Sparks fly from the rails about four feet below. The grit and flying cinders at 75 miles an hour make me forget the beating of my heart. I wonder if Bob is safely aboard and if he knows where I am.

The Chief stops for just a minute or two at the junction with Santa Fe. Under station lights, while many hobos are leaving, I have time to reunite with Bob. We hardly get a chance to talk before the Chief is speeding off again. I really did ride the blind but Bob's place is much safer. The temperature is cooling as we reach the higher elevations. Bob and I manage to sleep a bit. We each carry a large red handkerchief with us. Tonight we will use them to cover our mouths and noses during the ten or twelve minute ride through Raton Tunnel. The soot, steam and darkness are so terrifying that one of the hobos with us goes berserk. In a nightmarish scene, he goes wild and threatens to run out of this place. It takes five of us to restrain him. After that the sound of the engine becomes quiet. It puts us to sleep as we coast down the eastern slope.

"Come on, Martin! We overslept!" Bob shouts. "We must get off this train or ride into Kansas." We are already picking up speed, but Bob swings into his jump and is gone. Afraid of being hurt, I loiter too long. But I know I must jump so I grab the bar. My right foot is on the step. Swinging my left leg in the direction I will fall, I let go telling myself to "go limp." I roll head over heels in the cinders three times, then see Bob coming toward me about two blocks behind. I shake the ashes out of my hair. By this time, we are out in the country parallel to a highway. Two ladies give us a ride to La Junta and leave us at a cafe where we can wash up and get coffee.

Bob and I lose no time in spotting a string being set for Pueblo. That guarantees that we will get to Denver by tonight. But we arrive too late to catch the last car of the evening to Golden, so we walk. Bob and I are too happy to be tired. Ten miles seem longer in the dark, so we talk to pass the time. When we pass a cemetery on the left side of the road, Bob asks, "How many people do you think are dead there?" I give the usual "I don't know" answer. We break out in laughter when Bob says, "All of them."

In that spirit of happiness, we head for the 24-hour open house in Golden. It is kept by several faculty members for students needing a place to stay overnight in an emergency. There are no mosquitoes so all the doors are open. We drop on the first bed we find. But we stay there for only a minute. There is movement in our beds. In the past ten days we have slept in many places, only to find the enemy when we are almost home. When Bob turns on the lights, we see bed bugs everywhere. They are even crawling up the walls! We go out on the porch and lie down on the floor. We barely get through assuring each other that there will be no freight car coupling and crashing tonight when both of us are asleep.

Shortly after eight o'clock, we are awakened by a Western Union messenger with a telegram from my sister reporting that she and my father had been in a car accident. My father is in the hospital in Aberdeen. I borrow the price of coach fare on the Milwaukee and hurry home where I find my "Pappy" well on the mend.

After a few minutes of happy hugs, kisses and greetings, what do you think is the first question he asks me?

* * *

Epilogue

My father and mother both died at the conclusion of World War II. They lie buried in the Lutheran Cemetery at Springfield, Minnesota.

In the wide open, extensive, flat area between the crossroads at Vincent and the crossroads at Gail in Borden County, Texas, there is an outstandingly high and lonely hill. It is called Gail Mountain. A very large star has been constructed atop this hill. When lighted at Christmas time it can be seen for many miles away. The annual lighting of the star has always been in commemoration of the Christian heritage of the area. This year, an enlarged star will shine also in honor and tribute to those persons no longer living whose names appear early in the Book of Records.

Because my father's name appears in those Records, I was contacted last fall. A donation was requested and I was asked whether I wished to have Father's name inscribed among those for whom the star will shine some night during the Christmas season.

I don't believe that Gail Mountain is more than eight or ten miles from the area to which Mr. Von Roeder took Bob Swancutt and me on a rabbit hunt that afternoon sixty-four years ago. At one point during the hunt, he shut off the motor and said very plainly, "This can't be more than a mile from where your Pappy owns a piece of the ground."

What a rare opportunity this is for my family and me to pay tribute to our father and mother who lived with a hope and a tease concerning a small patch of ground which neither of them would ever see.

May the light of that star on Gail Mountain shine very brightly on that little piece of the earth this Christmas.

THE LAST PARSONAGE

It was not easy to leave friends who had become dear to us in the eight years of living with them in Moline, Illinois. It was not easy to say goodbye to the Mississippi River and the Hennepin Canal in which we used to swim with the water moccasins and scold at the biting chiggers. The farther west the 1940 Chevie with trailer attached took Alma, Mary and me, the more we were looking forward with anticipation to our new venture. We were free of the stress and the drive that prevail in the farm implement manufacturing capital of the world. We were going out to where those implements were being used. Not only that: Alma and I were going back to the profession in which we had met each other some ten years before, namely that of teaching.

The roads had been good all the way, but on the second day, only an hour and a half to the end of our 750 mile trip, the road branched south on #40 and then, after a few miles the gravel-surfaced highway, came to an end. The rest of the way to Scenic, our destination, we drove on a dry, tan gumbo dirt road. A member of the school board had arranged for our living quarters until the moving van could bring our furniture.

The next morning we were shown the place where we were to make our home, a large, two story, stately older house. It had a covered porch in the front and a covered porch in the back also. Nearby was a shed and still farther, an outhouse. When we came closer, the once grand home showed us results of its age and dilapidation. Loose boards stood out on all sides and evidence of paint had withered away long ago. Windows were loose and without screens. But somehow, we sensed that it demanded respect because it was the Parsonage. We could see the school to the south. Leaving the car, we walked in that direction. From a distance, the building looked like a large cement box with windows.

It was held upright by means of large iron bolts which ran the length and breadth of the building, guarding against the frequent slippage of the earth. Inside, the school identified itself properly, but the desk-tops and floors gave away its age. It was here that Alma and I would spend much of the next nine months. This is what we came here for.

The first day of school, with only the usual registration in the forenoon, had gone well. In that spirit, we were arranging the furniture which the van had left at the parsonage at noon. Suddenly, without a knock, a man with a silver badge came through the door and in a loud voice directed at me, commanded me to drop everything and come with him. He told me there was a fire on Kube Table and handed me a gunny sack, saying that the water barrel was on his truck. He was the Fire Marshal, so without even removing my tie, I was on the truck with others on my way to fight the fire. I was certain that from one of those clumps of buffalo grass a rattlesnake would strike at me or my gunny sack.

As the days at school passed, activity gained momentum. I was superintendent of the staff of five. On the day that the first checks of the year were ready, I decided on my morning trip to the Post Office to pick them up from the treasurer, who was also the owner of the saloon across the street. As he came back from the safe with a brown envelope, he reached below the bar for a small glass which he set in front of me. Waving to the assortment of liquor on his shelf, he asked "What's your pleasure?" I was astonished and thanked him quite properly, but explained that this was school time and that I thought it would be improper for me to drink while on duty. I took the brown envelope with the checks, but left with the feeling that by refusing his drink, I had refused his hand of friendship.

There were extra-curricular duties expected of me of which I was not aware. Things that the other superintendents had taken care of soon became a custom for them and were now expected of me. The township hall was the site of a public dance every last

Saturday of the month. One day, I was asked whether I had gotten a band for the next dance. I was as surprised at this point as I was with my treasurer. Of course, I had to answer in the negative. I also conveyed my understanding that I had come here to manage the school. No more was said about this. Monthly dances went on as usual; people looked forward to them. There was very little community recreational activity in which all people could participate except for this dance. Superintendents should be there to help. Would I learn?

One Saturday that fall the storekeeper took me out to one of the tables infested with prairie dogs. We kept our rifles busy until we were out of cartridges. When we came back, he invited me into the store. There were chairs in the corner and I sat down to think over the great shoot. Then the storekeeper brought two pints of ice cream, one of which he handed to me. When I asked for a knife with which to cut the container in half because I was not accustomed to so much at one time, he took the container from me, saying that anyone who couldn't eat a pint of ice cream didn't deserve any. Then he put it back in the freezer. We talked of other things until a man wearing a double layer of overalls under a much worn, heavy, dusty jacket, and a large, dark, western felt hat came into the store. When it came to paying the bill for his groceries, he reached into his hip pocket and came out with a large roll of bills. He must have picked the wrong roll, because he quickly put it back. While mumbling to himself he reached into the pocket on the other side and came out with a roll as large as the first. He pulled a bill out of this one, waited for change and walked out. When I wondered who had that much money to be walking around with, I was told that wasn't all of it. The rich man's daughter attended our school. If he had put all of his white-faced cattle on the market, he could have settled nearly a half million dollars in the bank. He had bought an electric washer for his wife, which lasted only a short while on the south side of the house where it still remained. It was full of sand every week.

To go to the Post Office for mail or to buy groceries, we had to walk past the township jail. The jail and the parsonage were featured in the April 1981 National Geographic magazine. The walls of the jail were at least three feet thick. They were made of a special cement and large stones. It had four windows about 18 inches square into which opening iron rods were secured in the building walls. There was no glass for protection. The building was about 24 feet square. The door was of welded sheet steel, and the lock was one of a kind. Only one man knew the code to the lock.

By Thanksgiving time we wanted to get out for a day or so. Disregarding the weather reports for west of the Missouri, we enjoyed the start of the trip. But our brother-in-law met us in Arlington, helped us through the snow and ice and got us to Hayti at near midnight. During the next two days there was some thawing and with daylight now on our side, we wasted no time starting for home. We were happy to get back to our place that evening. It was our home in the heart of the South Dakota Bad Lands, just a couple miles north of the Pine Ridge Indian Reservation and only 28 miles north of Wounded Knee. When we left Moline, we did not know the location of our new home. At the time, we only knew we were going to Scenic.

There were two churches in our town of Scenic, one Catholic and one for the Protestants. Various clergy would come from Rapid City at announced times and conduct well attended Sunday evening services. After the service, the pastors would usually stop for coffee and cake and visit with us. It seemed like a Sunday evening at home years ago.

Christmas is celebrated in remote areas also. Alma planned and rehearsed a school program for Christmas that would include every child in the school. Songs and skits and dialog and readings were part of the program. I would make the setting more memorable by bringing in a fresh, aromatic cedar from the breaks near Sheep Mountain. I had a boy with a pickup help me. The one I chose for the school was under five feet, but the two of us could hardly handle it. We even found a smaller one for our house. What a Christmas! Choosing our own tree from nature was great! People began coming early for the program. They kept coming until the little auditorium left many standing. The program was well accepted and aroused happy feelings in the people. A change in their spirit was evident in their well wishes and chatter before they started for home.

Alma and I went home, too, with our Mary. We had our small tree set up with a little tinsel and a few lights. We could hardly wait until we would lead Mary out from the kitchen with her hands covering her eyes until her present was before her. A red wagon! A very happy Christmas for us all.

I learned how sturdy, strong and heavy those cedar trees are that one sees while driving past them in the breaks of the Badlands and how slow their rate of growth is. I also learned that it is against the law for anyone to enter the Bad Lands and take any of its nature with him when he leaves.

A couple of days after the high of Christmas, nostalgia took over again and we decided to try a trip to Casper, Wyoming where Alma had a sister. This time it was wind and snow on the way home. We were glad to get back to our place. It was the last day of the year – New Year's Eve! People were already coming into town to celebrate. There would be a New Year's Eve dance in the township hall. Usually in the evening the town became dark, but tonight the area around township hall was very bright all around. It gets sort of lonesome when lights are out and you can hear music and imagining fun that is not far away. We finally dressed Mary and ourselves and walked over to the township hall. How glad we were! Everyone seemed to be there and everyone wore a happy face. Twenty-four-inch benches were built into the south and west walls of the hall where the very young and sleeping children could rest. Those that remained awake toddled around with the ones dancing. Mary enjoyed herself. The behavior of the crowd was to be commended, possibly because of the rule in the township hall. Improper behavior was shown the door early, regardless of whether the offender was white or Native American. I even promised to arrange for a dance band for the last three dances of the year.

Alma's busy schedule of a school program and regular classes was a greater load than she should have been responsible for. A short week into February she woke me at one o'clock at night. I hurried to dust some snow from the foot of the bed, dressed quickly and carried Mary over to a near neighbor. Then Alma and I sped off to Rapid City. Drifting snow made it hard to drive and I could not avoid hitting a porcupine. After being assured that Alma would be well taken care of, I returned to Scenic to call a substitute and start the day as usual. At about 6:30, I got the happy call that baby Annie had been born. The porcupine was the cause of a flat tire a week later.

Because of the small enrollment, Scenic had Commencement Exercises every other year. One boy was waiting to graduate. I didn't believe he ought to waste a whole year, so I put him in line with an extension course plus private tutoring. He did not get true or false tests, but his answers to questions came in a very intelligent essay. I went to Rapid City and asked a local state politician to help with a commencement address, but he didn't have time for even a greeting from me. I went to call on the Editor of the Rapid City Journal who listened to my story. After calling a secretary to make note of the details of time and place, he rose, held out his right hand and told me not to worry. "That boy is going to have a commencement!" he promised.

At noon on the appointed day, the editor called me. At five o'clock that afternoon an Associated Press Photography unit came into town. At 7:30, the editor was there, ready to give the address himself. The picture of that single graduate appeared in all American newspapers that subscribed to A. P. photo news. Another boy, who was a Junior that year, is now a Doctor of Philosophy at the University of Vancouver.

I know that I will always be able to identify myself as a P. K. I am proud of the years of my youth that I was able to spend with my folks in a parsonage. The episodes that I have mentioned in this account are but a few of the many that have stayed in my memory of the year that my family and I lived in a parsonage and they may be the last that I write with the background of a parsonage. It was 1947. But I'm happy that these stories come from our living in the venerable old Parsonage in Scenic, South Dakota.

Missionaries spend much time and energy doing their work and are happy when they can say that they have served even one. We were missionaries in a different arena, but we are just as happy to know that one student made it to graduation, and that another had been made ready for the next year.

> *In Calgary, when I was very young, I learned to like peppermint candy. The kind men who came to see Papa were usually wearing grubby, none-too-clean work clothes. When I came near, they would reach into their overall or jacket pocket and pull out a grayish colored disk of peppermint candy. Those treats never came from a sack or box. They were mingled with anything else that happened to be stored in their pocket. It didn't make much difference to me, but Mama would be standing in the door cringing, watching to be sure that I said "dankeschoen." She was probably glad that Mr. Repp was not carrying chewing tobacco.*

CHRISTMAS AT HOME

On this, my 89th year, I look back and review what I learned and was taught about the observance of Christmas. I understand more fully the depth of the reasons for the way we prepared for Christmas to come at our house. The secrecy and supervision were my parents in partnership. When the oldest sisters became aware of the mystery surrounding the event, they became helpers for the parents, thus making the waiting and watching for any signs even greater and much more exciting.

We had Christmas poetry, songs and skits to learn for the program in the Mitchell County School which we attended. We also had songs and verses to learn and sing for the program in church on Christmas Eve. At the end of that program all of the children were given a large candy-striped sack of candy, nuts and peanuts and an orange.

When the church program was over and our family had all gotten together, we children were left in the kitchen behind the closed door to the parlor. We were to be orderly and quiet because Papa and Mama would have to let das Christkind in at the front door. Christmas music was coming from a record on the Victrola, while the tree was being brought in from its hiding place in the master bedroom. It had been decorated just that afternoon while we were taking a nap for over an hour to prepare for the long evening ahead. The tree would now be set up in the front room.

We had to wait patiently for our expectations were great. When everything was ready, Mama came in, blindfolded each child and then led us into the front room where Papa would help place each child behind the gifts which were around the tree. As we stood there blindfolded, hardly able to wait any longer, we sang "Alle Jahre Wieder" once more. Then we could remove the blinds.

What an outburst of joy and happiness, of cheers, thanks and other expressions of love! How did das Christkind know what I wanted?

After we had compared our gifts and become quieter, most likely because we were reading in one of the books we had received, Papa would light several of the wax candles on the tree. Mama would turn the gas lamp real low. We would sing "Stille Nacht" once more and then everyone went to bed.

When we came down on festive Christmas Day morning, all was as we had left it the night before, but on the round table between the tree and the piano was a large fold-open creche of that first Christmas.

That was the way, with necessary adaptations, that I learned to observe Christmas with my parents when I was growing up. Alma and I have used that same pattern in our celebrations with our children when they were growing up. For us, these celebrations seem to have focused on three aspects of Christmas: Secrets, Sacrifice and Song.

* * *

Secrets

When the youngest of our children, Max, was old enough to have a desire for an electric train, he was also coming to the point of losing his innocence concerning Christmas gifts and das Christkind. He kept up his hopes about the electric train, but he did not want his parents to know that he had doubts.

And so Christmas Eve came. During our ceremony, he was in high spirits like the rest of us. Max was made extremely happy when, sure enough, there was that electric train that he had wanted. It was more beautiful than he had expected. He was eager for floor space tomorrow where he could set up his train.

A few days later while he was sitting at the kitchen eating a snack, he said to Alma, "Mom, you should have hidden that train better. I found it before Christmas." He had done a good job of covering up for us, but the surprise for him was gone.

Sacrifice

During the last of her grade school years, our older daughter, Mary took advantage of baby-sitting. It was an opportunity to earn money for herself by taking care of neighborhood children. Some of those evenings got to be long, especially when she had to call home and ask Alma what she could do for the crying baby that had a rash. These jobs did not pay very much, but over time, she had what she thought to be a tidy sum of money.

One afternoon during vacation, just before Christmas, a large crate sealed with wire was delivered to our front porch. It was labeled "Fancy Florida Grapefruit." When Mary saw it and realized what it was, she jumped and cheered for joy. "It is your Christmas present," she repeated several times. It was a proud moment for her. We were overwhelmed and a little abashed. Mary had no idea how large the present would be, but she was sure that the porch would be a good place to keep the fruit while we used it. It would not fit under the tree.

We found out later that Mary had used nearly all of her "own" money that she had earned up to that time. Did she get a dress or shoes? No. She spent $25 on a present for her parents with the first money she ever earned.

* * *

Song

Our whole family was in school daily and so it was an exception when Alma would get out her best dishes and call us together for the usual oyster stew and a sandwich at Christmas time. In the glow of the four Advent candles we were quietly tying our bonds as a family a bit tighter. Then we would say the Lord's Prayer together. The table would be cleaned, chairs put back, everything would have to be in order because this was Christmas Eve. But meanwhile, Hannelore had slipped upstairs.

When she thought everything was ready, she came down full of joy, beaming with happiness and handed each of us a copy of the program she would conduct. We would start with a song or two. A special reading for Alma followed, then a solo or a duet. The reading of the story in Luke was assigned to me, then Max would blow his trumpet, followed by some more singing. Hannelore was so spirited that she captivated us all. But when it came to her brother's turn to select a song, he demurred a bit and said, wondering, "When do we get to the presents?"

But we got to them, too. When all the gifts had been picked up, Alma came with dishes once more; cold cuts, cheese, crackers, Christmas cookies and herring were there. When everything had been cleaned up, we sang "Stille Nacht" once more. Then we went to bed.

ANECDOTES

I had just celebrated my tenth birthday when Papa accepted a call to serve a parish in northern South Dakota in McPherson County. I went from a country school class of two and was registered in a class of about twenty students. That first Friday afternoon was a happy time for me. I was on my way home to report much good news. Suddenly, during my short pass across an empty lot, I felt as though someone was behind me. When I heard my name called out, I turned to respond. At that moment, a large fist landed unceremoniously on my nose. I recognized the assailant as a member of my class. This was the way a newcomer was initiated at that school and my attacker was the enforcer.

Preachers' sons were not allowed to indulge in any disorderly conduct. Papa had instructed me to keep out of trouble and even though I had gotten to the point of depending on myself when I was bullied, I would still have to go home with blood running down my face. I hated the names they called me like "Dutchy, Kaiser or Hun," but those cruel names didn't bother me as much as being called "fraidy cat." During noon hour and after school, we in the grade school played marbles. In the spring, when I was in the eighth grade, an argument started. I happened to participate because the fight was about my snotagate. I had offended the butcher's son by responding to his insulting names with one of my own. He demanded that I take it back, but I refused. He had bullied me for too long!

High school classes had just let out and the boys smelled trouble. They soon encircled us. I could find no route for escape and I was scared. In that moment my sense of decorum was forgotten and my anger took over completely. In desperation, I took offense with a vengeance. Without thinking or reasoning, I grabbed my opponent by his hair, or whatever else I could get hold of, and knocked him on his rear. I repeated this process several times, then told him to go home.

My victory left me in high spirits. I don't remember what happened to the marble game, or the crowd that had gathered to see the fight, but there were no more insulting names, and I was not hurt or bleeding. I started slowly to walk home, wondering what I would say to Papa about having been in a fight. But before I got home, a neighbor who had witnessed the affair stopped by to congratulate my father for having a son that would finally teach "that boy" a lesson. That man didn't even belong to our church. So in the eyes of my father, I became a sort of hero. The next morning, my opponent of the day before came to school with a black eye, two yellow cheeks and one arm in a sling. Because the action had taken place on school grounds, I was called upstairs to the Superintendent's office for what I took for a scolding

※ ※ ※

Four of us ninth graders had gotten to know one another and formed our own little group. On that Halloween night, we decided not to go with the gang. We would do something different. Barney Friedman had some cattle in the holding yard waiting to be shipped out. The cattle buyer had just had a load of corn stalk bundles hauled in to feed the cattle before loading.

When we had unloaded the rack of cattle feed, we were happy with what we had done. We had played our trick without bothering a single outhouse. Most other boys wished that they had gone with us. A minute past nine, the next morning, all of the boys were called into the music room. The Superintendent asked "Now which one of you boys helped empty Barney Friedman's rack of corn bundles?" First four, then six, then eleven boys raised their hand. The rest were dismissed. "Now, you go down during the noon hour and re-load those corn stalks onto the rack where they were," he ordered sternly. Fortunately, Barney just laughed about the event. "Those kids were scared of the cattle, so they unloaded the corn on the dry side," he said. "They're very lucky, because otherwise I would have had a lot of bloated and dead cattle." We didn't know much about that, but we were glad that we had seven unexpected helpers at re-loading the feed corn.

* * *

After living in Iowa for the entire period of World War I, we moved to a little town in north central South Dakota which maintained an accredited four year high school. The parsonage, which was two blocks from the church, was situated between two large houses in which country German was still spoken. Sometimes the neighbors would become very loud. One spring Sunday afternoon, Mama and I were at our back door. I listened for a bit. Then, before we knew what was happening, a half full coal scuttle came flying out through the window of the unopened back door. That delayed the entry of the husband who was trying to get in, long enough for him to shout in a loud voice, "Now, Emma, you old blood-sausage!" I don't know what happened then because Mama said "We better get into our own house!!

* * *

When directors were selected to oversee the liquidation of one of the banks that had closed because of the depression, one of those selected was a county officeholder who had a great knowledge of the bank's holdings. The other director was my father. He was appointed because he was the most trustworthy and honest man they could find. Those two men had been deeply antagonistic toward each other for many years, but during the course of the liquidation meetings, a reconciliation between them took place and they became friends.

* * *

If prospects looked good for the ranchers in the spring, a lot of cattle was shipped by railroad cattle cars from the south and unloaded at the west end of the tracks. They were fed for a day and then the huge herd would be driven out to the rancher who would take care of them until fall when they would be reloaded once more. By this time they were ready to be sent to the slaughterhouse in St. Paul. It was fun to watch the cowboys keep all of the animals together as they herded them right through town. We thought the cowboys on their beautiful horses, wearing big hats and leather chaps and cracking their whips were great. We played cowboys for a long time after watching those drives.

* * *

Two members of the congregation were at odds with each other. Finally one filed a law suit against the other. At about one o'clock at night, the day before the trial was to start, four men came to the front door and asked to lay out their case before my dad. They were in the front room just next to the open staircase to the second floor where I had been awakened by them. I could hear their claims against each other in the upper decibels of their voices. Finally, after about an hour, there came a quieting of the words followed by sobs of forgiveness and remorse. The two antagonists began shaking hands and promising friendship to each other. They prayed the Lord's Prayer together and that was the end of the law suit. When the public heard what happened to the upcoming court case, they asked what Papa had charged for his services. Everyone was amazed when they learned he charged nothing for arbitrating the cases. The lawyers were the only ones who suffered. They had gotten beat out of their fees.

* * *

When I was 12 or 13 years old, I would go out to the garage in the cold winter months, jack the right rear axle of the car, release the hand clutch and then run back to the house and bring out a kettle of hot water to pour over the in-take manifold. Then I would go to the front of the Ford and pull up on the crank. If I choked it just right, the car would start on the second or third pull. If not, I would have to go through the procedure again. Either way, we always got Lizzie started. Then I would pull up the hand clutch, remove the special jacks, open the garage door, back the car out and get ready to go the 12 miles with Papa to the Hope congregation where he conducted services every other Sunday morning. Sometimes it was very cold, maybe four degrees below zero or lower.

* * *

In our little town it was permissible to maintain a cow to supply milk for our family of six children. I didn't mind school, but in the spring, I was happy to get home in the afternoon, hook our cow, Blume, to the 25 foot chain and lead her out beyond the city limits to graze on the prairie grass. That time gave me the opportunity to sit or lie with my back to the ground and think about the everlasting life of the May-fly or the worries of the gopher. Then I would pull the stake that held the 25 foot chain and Blume and I would go home. I would have a fistful of May flowers to bring to my mother. I later learned that the flowers were pasque flowers. In Calgary, we called them crocus.

* * *

The older German-Russians had a hard time catching on to some of the common English expressions. In the corner grocery/dry goods store where I worked one summer, we sold from a separate shed in the alley, kerosene for ordinary lamps, and high test gasoline for pressure lamps and for dry cleaning clothes at home. We called what we put into the cars gas, and they called it "gessoline." When a customer told me he wanted "gaas" I gave him a quart of high test gasoline. Next morning, before the store was open, he was there wanting to know what I had given him. I looked at Lyle who was sweeping the sidewalk with me as the man continued again, "Wat you give me exploded my lamp all to pieces."

* * *

By sending to fur buying companies that advertised the highest prices for any fur, and "sure-catch" supplies for any trapper, I received mail throughout the winter. My fantasy of trapping larger animals than gophers came true when I caught a muskrat when I was a first grader at Tesch's school, for which an older boy gave me 50 cents. I did however get to skin a skunk later. That netted me $1.50.

* * *

During the dry years most of the economy of the country hit bottom. During one of the first years that I worked for a farmer, I drove a lumber wagon loaded with two 250 pound hogs to town one day. The farmer was credited with less than ten dollars for the two prime pigs. The wagon was powered by two fine horses, but the round trip of 20 miles, 10 each way, took almost all day. I earned one dollar for this job.

* * *

Farmers would wait in the house until about 10:30 or 11:00 o'clock in the morning. Then there would come three long rings on the phone. That would be the market report. Everything was fine, the wheat and cattle market didn't mean so much to my dad, and when it came to "swine," he heard "time". He could not see why his "clock" was never right one day to the next.

* * *

It seemed that the rites and practices of the aging members of Protestant denominations were giving way to outside influences which allowed some members of secret organizations to become leaders of Protestantism. Lutherans were uniformly against this intrusion because it allowed and helped in the disintegration of hope and trust in the original body.

* * *

We children soon found out that my dad had an aversion to blood and could not behead a rooster with a hatchet in order to have chicken for a meal. Although Mother was raised on a farm in Ohio, it was the custom there that one of the sons would kill the fowl. So my dad bought a shot gun with which he could do the deed at least a bit out of sight.

* * *

When Dad was invited by parishioners to come along on a hunting trip, he explained that he was never a hunter, but he let them know that he had a 12 gauge repeater upstairs in a closet.

Some time later, one of the deacons came to ask whether he could borrow that gun for a Canadian goose hunt on a lake about 50 miles east of home. Certainly Dad could not refuse with the promise of a goose. That gun was not brought back for a long time, but when it was returned, it was bright and shiny. The goose had been cooked a while back. I learned later, overhearing a bit of humor in the barber shop, that the shotgun had been dropped into the lake on the day of the shooting and had to be retrieved by making a special trip bringing special equipment to fish "the preacher's gun out of the lake."

* * *

During the 30's, the years of the drought, there was so little food in the pasture and hay fields that the cattle were starving and feed for them had to be shipped in. But without a crop of wheat or corn, farmers had no resources for money. There was no way for them to maintain their herds. Hundreds of month-old calves were brought to the slaughter pits where under government supervision, they were shot and buried in long trenches. There simply was not enough feed to sustain their lives.

* * *

During the time when calves were slaughtered because of lack of feed, the government allowed some of the meat to be saved and brought to people who could use it immediately since refrigerators were not yet in use. A hind quarter of one of these young calves was brought to our house during that time. My mother could not quite justify this to herself. Although this calf had been saved from the pits, it had to die because the owner did not have enough food and now we were to eat of it.

* * *

Driving through the country, one often saw small sod houses, some with an add-on and beside it a large white house, usually two stories with an attic, square and with a basement. This usually reflected the prosperity of the owner, both financially and their need for a bigger house to rear a family.

* * *

The early settlers and farmers settled their first heating problem by roaming the prairie searching for remaining buffalo chips. Then, to save time walking through their cattle pastures, they added a side industry to their cream sales. Driving through that area one was often surprised by the sweet aroma which the wind carried across the prairie. In the direction from which the wind was coming, you could say for certain that some housewife was baking bread. If you looked, you could see the neatly stacked squares of cultured cow chips near the house.

* * *

In all the years I can remember, the telephone in the parsonage was of the "hang on the wall" type, as were all home phones. The rural area was divided into "lines." Each line had a certain number of connected phones. Those on the line with you could call if they knew the "longs" and "shorts" to crank in the right sequence. The rings would alert everyone on that line and everyone could listen. It was a sort of "local news" at the source. The telephone wires were not insulated and after storms had torn them off the pole, they would ground out on the farmer's fence and the telephone system would no longer work. Most of the lines were corrected at first by tying them to an unbroken length of cattle fence barb wire on a wooden post. In dry weather, this worked for a while.

* * *

If suitable partners, for young people of marriageable age, could not find each other in the public association areas and meetings, it was always possible to engage a "Kupel Vater" (couple father). This person had lists of eligible men to which he would present, in buggy or other vehicle, a young lady to an eligible young man. If the two young people didn't move along too rapidly, a promise of a cow or a couple stacks of hay delivered by the father-in-law at the wedding would help. What commission the "couple-father" drew was never disclosed. If the first attempt was a failure, there were always others to try.

* * *

On a tour to the western part of the state to show a guest from Ohio how Indians lived on the Reservations, we were lucky enough to drive through a little Indian town where a great Pow Wow was in progress. On the way home, we drove past a typical Indian farm home and stopped in to talk to the man walking in the yard. We asked him why he wasn't at the Pow Wow, to which he answered, "Government gave me land. They get money. I have land."

* * *

There were about 22 students in my eighth grade class. I had a seat in just about the center of the square room. My neighbor across the aisle was a bit taller than I. I'd had nothing to do with him since we first met. I certainly didn't like him, but was sorry for him because I'd recently learned his brother-in-law had just been convicted of a murder and been sent to the penitentiary. He was the boy that had given me the bloody nose that Friday several years ago.

* * *

It was not unusual for a farmer to spot a coyote on his way to town. The local veterinary was the first to be notified. He would drop everything when he received the call, load up two or three of his blood hounds, and speed the six blocks to the Barber Shop. Lon, the Barber, might be in the middle of shaving the butcher or the County Judge, but he would drop everything and take off with Doc and the dogs on a fun trip across the prairie. I always had my hair cut by Lon's brother in the other chair.

* * *

People who lived on a farm were satisfied that their future rested with that property. A family of one son would inherit the farm, marry and establish a family. If there were two sons, it was up to the father to have at least an extra quarter of farm land to leave to the second son. The farm family that had four sons was hard put, but the father usually managed to have title to enough land so each son could start a place of his own. Any girls in the area looked for one of these young men, someone with whom they could start a place of their own.

* * *

Having become one of the most successful farmers of the area after World War I, one of our friends who had four sons, lost everything beginning with the end of the 1920's, followed by the dry 30's. After trying to save a part of his land, even the homestead was given up in mortgage. After the banks and the insurance companies and whoever else had a lien on the livestock or the machinery were satisfied, there wasn't a penny left for this man who had once had the world before him. He finally went to Oregon and got a job in a pea cannery.

* * *

The glacier of centuries earlier had dropped many rocks and stones when it receded. Most of them showed above the virgin prairie, and when the farmer wanted to break a new piece of land for cultivation, he went about it with a team of horses pulling a stone boat to which was attached a light cart or wagon. With this he went from one area of the new field to the other, picking up the rocks and loading them on the stone boat. The buffalo chips he put in the little light wagon. The rocks were unloaded at a corner of the field and the cow droppings or chips were taken home and stacked some place near to the kitchen door.

* * *

When we lived in Calgary, Canada prior to World War I, we had a bathroom with a flush toilet in our house. The reservoir was five or more feet high, above the stool on the wall. It was operated with a pull chain. We lost that facility when we moved back to north central Iowa. There, small towns put on special police to keep vandals from tipping over the unguarded out-houses on Halloween night.

* * *

There was a yearly period right after the close of the regular public schools in the area for all the boys and girls who were getting prepared for Confirmation. This instruction was conducted by the St. James Parish. The sessions lasted for five weeks and attendance was required for two successive years.

* * *

Big cars would often come into town from the west at high speeds, barely slowing down as they passed through. There was growing traffic on Highway 10, the shortest route to Minnesota and east. It was common knowledge that these cars belonged to bootleggers or booze runners who delivered liquor to points east. The booze, mostly grain alcohol, was made in the hill country north and west of town. The cars could be spotted by their heavy load. Even though they were equipped with special springs and shocks, the heavy, overloaded look of the cars gave them away.

* * *

The rules of the culture in our time, were fairly uniform. Whether people lived in a little town or on a farm, family life consisted of the husband supplying the cash to support his family while the wife took care of the household necessities needed to raise the children and care for her husband.

* * *

If a father needed to miss a recreational activity with the other men in order to help clean up dishes or take care of their baby more often than was thought proper, he was considered and talked of as being hen-pecked.

* * *

On the farm, cows had to be milked and the rest of the livestock had to be cared for. These were routine jobs that occurred every twelve hours. But whether in the country or in town, the noon meal was dinner and the evening meal was supper. You could tell people from outside the farming area by how they referred to these meals. If they asked for dinner in the evening, they were obviously foreigners.